instrumentality n. 手段；工具；部
instrumental adj. 有幫助的；樂器

New TOEIC Listeni

 U0097858

instrument ① 樂器

② 手段；工具：Language is an instrument for communica....
③ 工具；機械 = implement; tool; utensil

PART 1

1. (A) (A) The man is standing with a musical <u>instrument</u>.
   - (B) The man is walking with a cane. *① 莖 ② 柺杖 v. 打：If you say*
   - (C) The man is pushing a shopping cart. *it again, you'll get*
   - (D) The man is reading a newspaper. *caned.*

at seize

2. (A) (A) The office is unoccupied.
   - (B) The station is congested. *v. 充滿；阻塞；充血*
   - (C) The sidewalk is obstructed. *carry ⇒ congestion*
   - (D) The desks are in a circle. *against build v. 阻礙；防礙*

   ⇒ obstruction n. 障礙物
   封鎖

3. (C) (A) Some people are swimming in the ocean.
   - (B) Some people are watching a musical performance.
   - (C) Some people are sitting on park benches.
   - (D) Some people are bathing in a fountain.

① bathe v. 弄溼 ① Will you help me
bathe the baby?

4. (B) (A) A few people are waiting in line.
   - (B) A large crowd has gathered outdoors. *② Her eyes were*
   - (C) A building is on fire. *bathed in tears.*
   - (D) An actor is giving a speech. *淚眼汪汪*

   deliver / make
   ③ be bathed in
   = be covered with

5. (D) (A) A child is playing with a toy.
   - (B) A chef is giving a demonstration.
   - (C) A doctor is writing a prescription. (下)
   - (D) A man is speaking in front of an audience. *write*

6. (A) (A) The man is operating a piece of heavy machinery.
   - (B) A woman is doing laundry.
   - (C) A boy is reading a book.
   - (D) A girl is <u>applying</u> <u>makeup</u> to her face.

＊ prescribe v. 規定；開處方 ⇒ prescription n. 處方
1921

prescript n. 命令；規定

prescriptive adj. 規定的；慣例的

proscribe v. 放逐；禁止 ⇒ proscription n. 放逐；禁止

GO ON TO THE NEXT PAGE

PART 2

聽力 5-2

7. (B) Where is the human resources department? 人力資源 部門
   (A) Yes, just a little bit.
   (B) Second door on the right.
   (C) Tickets are sold out already.

① be at the end of one's resources 智窮力竭
② a man of great resources 多計謀之人
③ natural resources 自然資源

8. (C) Why has our flight been rescheduled?
   (A) That won't be necessary.
   (B) He used to live near the airport.
   (C) There was a mechanical issue.

① 機械的
② 呆板的；無表情的；無意識的
   → Blinking is a mechanical action of the eyelids.
③ 手工操作的 ④ 技巧上的

9. (B) How long is Jeffery going to be out of the office?
   (A) No, the next one.
   (B) Until the end of the week.
   (C) A few kilometers.

10. (C) You're going to see Dr. Smith this morning, aren't you?
    (A) That's the new research laboratory.
    (B) Several other patients.
    (C) No, not until after lunch.

11. (C) Who's covering the press conference down at City Hall?
    (A) It's on the front page.
    (B) Around six o'clock.
    (C) Tom Tyler, most likely.

to/toward a point away from the speaker

12. (C) Would you care for a refill of your coffee?
    (A) In the break room.
    (B) The menu's on the table.
    (C) Thanks. Just half a cup.

= want   *care for ① 喜歡
② 照顧：The children are well cared for.
③ 計較：He does't care for what he eats.

13. (A) Why are you looking for more factory employees?
    (A) Our business has increased.
    (B) No, I didn't.
    (C) At the Valley Shopping Center.

employee of the month 本月最佳員工
engagement 員工認同

訂婚；諾言
→ The singer signed a contract for a two-year engagement.

14. (B) Where do you want me to save this computer file?
    (A) Monday at noon.
    (B) On the network server.
    (C) 5,000 dollars.

簽3兩年合約

15. (A) Please leave a copy of the report on my desk.
    (A) I'll do it before I leave tonight.
    (B) Do you have their phone number?
    (C) We just ordered 20 units.

16. (A) Have you met the new personnel director yet?
    (A) Yes, earlier this afternoon.
    (B) I'll send you an email.
    (C) They offered me a job.

人事主任

①人員；員工（幾稱）
②人事部門（課）

17. (C) There aren't enough chairs in the conference room.
    (A) Our seats are in the balcony.
    (B) It's scheduled for tomorrow evening.
    (C) I'll ask maintenance to bring out more.

18. (A) Do you want to introduce Ms. Riley, or should I?
    (A) Why don't you do it?   *紅*
    (B) Yes, I gave it to her.
    (C) That should work.

19. (A) I'd like to take this SUV for a test drive.
    (A) Let me get the keys.
    (B) I'll see her this afternoon.
    (C) Yes, 35 miles per gallon.

SUV:
sport utility vehicle
①效用
②公用事業（utilities）
adj. 費用的：多用途的

①車載工具：carriage
= conveyance
②手段方法：
Language is the vehicle of thought.
語言是表達思想的工具

20. (B) Who is closing tonight?
    (A) We close at midnight.
    (B) Jack is.
    (C) Put them in the freezer.

冷凍庫
a cold storage
a refrigerator
a cold store

21. (A) Has the Martin Supply Company order been shipped yet?
    (A) It went out yesterday.
    (B) It's my business card.
    (C) He's on line four.

①訂單：John's company received a large order for bags.
②秩序規律：Tina can't keep order in her class.
③狀況 = Things were in terrible order.

22. (C) I need to find an ATM on the way to the restaurant.
    (A) Will there be a refund?
    (B) No, not right now. Thanks.
    (C) But dinner is on me.

n. refund
v. refund

GO ON TO THE NEXT PAGE.

23. (A) Which candidate did Mr. Robertson hire?
    (A) He's still conducting interviews.
    (B) A bit higher than that.
    (C) Several excellent programs.

24. (C) Are the supervisors from the Los Angeles facility included in the meeting?
    (A) Up to 12 people.
    (B) The presentation was a little long.
    (C) Yes, they'll be arriving shortly.

25. (C) Does anybody have any ideas for the music festival?
    (A) We had a great time.
    (B) It was mainly classical music.
    (C) Yes, I have a lot of suggestions.

26. (C) What time is your meeting with Mr. Greeley?
    (A) No, I like the other one.
    (B) Once a month.
    (C) He cancelled.

27. (B) The main parking lot is always full by 9:00 a.m.
    (A) Thanks, I just bought it.
    (B) You can always use the lot across the street.
    (C) A monthly parking pass.

28. (A) Will this year's sales convention be held in Cleveland?
    (A) No, it's been moved to Chicago.
    (B) He's a proficient programmer.
    (C) I'd rather stay late and finish it.

29. (C) Didn't you order some color samples from the manufacturer?
    (A) I think neutral colors work best.
    (B) This quarter's budget deficit.
    (C) Their Web site was down.

30. (C) Is the new printer as complicated to use as it looks?
    (A) It looked fine to me.
    (B) I don't know when we got it.
    (C) It's similar to our previous model.

31. (B) Looks like we'll have to meet another day.
     (A) Did you find it yet?
     (B) Let's do it tomorrow.
     (C) There's one in the lobby.

聽力 5-3

PART 3

Questions 32 through 34 refer to the following conversation.

W : Mike, Ms. Laughlin just called about her order. She wants us to double the number of uniforms we're making for her restaurant staff.

M : That's great news. Has the deadline changed also?

W : Actually, she still wants the order to be finished by the end of July

M : Hmm.... That's a problem. There is no way we can make so many uniforms that quickly.

W : How about we hire some part-time tailors to help with this extra work?

M : Good idea. Can you get a list of names for me?   ＊tailor

32. (C) Where do the speakers most likely work? n. ① 裁縫師(男)
     (A) At a local restaurant.   = garment maker
     (B) At an travel agency.   = costumer
     (C) At a clothing manufacturer.   = dress maker (女)
     (D) At a laundry service.   = modiste (女)

v. 裁製；修改
→ The clinic tailors
its treatment to
individual needs.

33. (C) What problem does the man mention?
     (A) An item is too expensive.
     (B) A client cancelled an order.
     (C) A deadline is not realistic.
     (D) An employee is sick.

＊material

34. (C) How will the speakers solve the problem? adj ① 物質的 : material comforts
     (A) By negotiating with a business.   ② 重要的(法) : A material witness failed
     (B) By updating a Web site.   to appear in court.
     (C) By hiring additional staff.
     (D) By purchasing more material.   n. 材料
                                          資料
                                          文具 = Your writing materials are in the
Questions 35 through 37 refer to the following conversation between three speakers. top drawer

M : Hi, Ms. Morgan. Did Doctor Benedict ask you to schedule another appointment? of your desk.
Woman US : Yes, but I'll have to check my calendar at home.

GO ON TO THE NEXT PAGE.

patient ≠ passion n. 熱情；激情

熱♡ : Annie had a passion for music.

He is very patient with his patients.

M : You can now make appointment on our Web site if you have a patient account. Just log on and view the available times online.

n. 病人

大脾氣 : He broke into a violent passion.

Woman US : Great. Can you sign me up for an account? *adj. 耐心的*

M : Maria handles all registration. Maria, can you help Ms. Morgan set up a patient account on our Web site?

Woman UK : Certainly. If you have a mobile phone, we can do it now; or I can give you a printout with instructions to set up your account later.

印出的資料   into build   instruct v. 教授；教導；指示
instructive adj. 有益的

Woman US : I'll set it up later.

Woman UK : OK, here are the instructions. Please don't hesitate to call with any questions.

instructor 指導者，講師

35. (C) Where are the speakers?
    (A) At an electronics store.
    (B) At a library.
    (C) At a medical clinic.
    (D) At a bank.

professor
associate professor 副教授
assistant professor 助理教授

36. (D) According to the man, why should Ms. Morgan open an account?
    (A) To receive a free gift.
    (B) To fill a prescription.
    (C) To place an order.
    (D) To make an appointment.

⚹ Right you are! = You are correct!
⚹ There you are!

① Hi   =Here you are 給你
② May I have the red one? There you a
③ I should have listened to you.
*   There you are. 你看吧!*
⑪ He told me a lie.
*   There you are. 果真如此*

37. (B) What does Maria give to Ms. Morgan?
    (A) A membership card.
    (B) A set of instructions.
    (C) An application.
    (D) A resume.

Questions 38 through 40 refer to the following conversation.

W : There you are, Bill. I received your e-mail about the sales meeting this Wednesday afternoon. But I'll be meeting with the vice president of Underwood Associates at 2:00 p.m.

M : Oh, that's right. It totally slipped my mind that you had a meeting at Underwood. How long do you think it will take? *意外的忘了*

W : Probably 30 to 45 minutes. I have to review a contract with him. Is there any way that you could start the meeting later in the day?

M : Unfortunately, the rest of the team isn't free after 2:30 p.m. But if it's OK with you, I can just e-mail you the minutes to look over on your own. Contact me next week if you have any questions. *細節 ①瀏覽；仔細檢查 : The auditors are looking over the bank's boo*
②原諒   : The teacher looked over her student's fault.

38. (C) What is the problem?
    (A) A contract is incorrect.
    (B) A deadline has been missed.
    (C) There is a scheduling conflict.
    (D) There are no sales clerks available.

*conflict n. 衝突；鬥爭
conflict v.
strike

inflict v. ①施加 ②處以刑罰
infliction n. 痛苦

39. (A) What does the woman inquire about?
    (A) Postponing a meeting.
    (B) Arranging a teleconference.
    (C) Comparing competitors' prices.
    (D) Purchasing new software.

* inquire about / into 詢問；調查
for 求見: A mas has been inquiring for you at the office.
after 問候

40. (C) What does the man say he will do?
    (A) Speak with a supervisor.
    (B) Contact a client.
    (C) Send some materials.
    (D) Find some supplies.

* require + V-ing 需要 ① The roof requires repairing.
② My car requires servicing 檢修 at least once a year.

* supply
v. 供給；供應
n. ①.供: We have new supplies of coats.
②補給品(複) : Our medical supplies are running short.
: My dad has cut off the supplies.

Questions 41 through 43 refer to the following conversation.

M : Ms. Shepard. How does the stage look to you? Are all the props in the right places?

W : The stage arrangement is fine. But can you make sure that there'll be enough spot lighting? I want all the actors to be visible.

vid, vis = see adj. 明而易見的

M : Of course. But I'd rather do it when the cast is here so I can be sure the lighting is right.

W : OK, I'm meeting them for lunch, and then we're coming back here to rehearse the show this afternoon. We'll see you then.

* visual adj. 視覺的；真實的
visionary n. 幻想家
adj. 幻想的；不實際的；空想的
vision n. 幻想，夢想；洞察力；美景
v. 夢見

41. (A) Who most likely is the woman?
    (A) A theater director.
    (B) A costume designer.
    (C) A journalist.
    (D) A musician.

42. (B) What does the woman ask about?
    (A) Some seating assignments.
    (B) Some lighting.
    (C) A performance date.
    (D) A guest list.

GO ON TO THE NEXT PAGE

43. (C) What does the man say he would prefer to do?
   (A) Speak with a manager.
   (B) Conduct some background research.
   (C) Complete a task at a later time.
   (D) Ask for an actor to repeat a line.

Questions 44 through 46 *refer to the following conversation.*

大會

M : Jennifer, I was thinking about our travel plan for the business convention we're going to in San Diego. It's less than two weeks away. How are you getting to the airport from here?

W : Well, the three of us are all taking the same flight, so maybe we could ride together from the office to the airport. But we'll be gone for several days, so the cost of parking will really add up.

M : Right. You know, I think it's much cheaper to take a taxi.

W : That's a possibility. Let's ask Glenn what he thinks.

44. (B) What does the man say will take place in two weeks?
   (A) A grand opening celebration.
   (B) A professional conference.
   (C) An awards ceremony.
   (D) A training seminar.

45. (A) What does the woman say she is concerned about?
   (A) A parking fee.
   (B) A canceled flight.
   (C) An inconvenient location.
   (D) A hotel reservation.

46. (C) Why does the man say, "it's much cheaper to take a taxi"?
   (A) To complain about a price.
   (B) To correct a mistake.
   (C) To make a suggestion.
   (D) To express regret.

Questions 47 through 49 *refer to the following conversation.*

W : Thank you for agreeing to sit down with me for an interview, Mr. Brighton. The readers of Guitar World Magazine are anxious to hear about your company's plans for a new guitar manufacturing plant. n. 植物；工廠；設施　v. 種植；插入；設置

M : My pleasure, Ashley. Yes, Starlight Guitars will be opening a facility in Hartford, Connecticut soon. We currently have two plants in the state of New York. So, we're looking forward to expanding our production capabilities in the northeastern region.

W : That's great news for fans of Starlight Guitars. And when will the first guitar be built in the new factory?

M : If everything goes according to plan, the first guitar will roll off the production line in June.

(handwritten: 從…走/產出 strike sb. off the roll 降格 印出)

47. (C) Who most likely is the woman?
    (A) An artist.
    (B) A college professor.
    (C) A journalist.
    (D) A mechanic.

*(handwritten: * resident n. 居住者；駐外代表 adj. 居民的 again | sit 人 residence n. 官邸，住宅 n. * 房舍；居住者 resident = tenant = indweller ~ householder = inhabitant → inhabitation live n. 居住)*

48. (D) What is the main topic of the conversation?
    (A) An increase in costs.
    (B) Customer reviews.
    (C) New guitar designs.
    (D) The opening of a factory.

49. (B) According to Mr. Brighton, what will happen in June?
    (A) An album will be recorded.
    (B) Production will begin at a facility.
    (C) Discounted instruments will be available.
    (D) An advertising campaign will start.

(handwritten: discount 5% for cash payment 現金付款 95折 discountable 可折價的)

Questions 50 through 52 *refer to the following conversation.*

W : Hello, Mr. Thompson. Welcome to AllBike Consulting. I was thrilled when I heard that a councilman from the City of Darien wanted to meet with us.

(handwritten left margin: 議員；委員 書記；評審 鑑賞)

M : Gee, thanks! The city council knows your company helps cities set up their bike share programs and Darien wants to establish one, too.

W : The concept is growing in popularity. What are your goals for your program?

M : We want to encourage our residents to exercise as well as to reduce car traffic, but it's going to be an uphill battle convincing people to participate.

(handwritten: 住於高處的；艱難的   合夥；搭檔)

W : That's where AllBike comes in. When cities partner with us, part of the service we provide is an advertising campaign. We'll produce television and radio commercials that will encourage community members to use the bikes.

*(handwritten: * popularity)*

50. (A) Who is the man?
    (A) A city official.
    (B) A television producer.
    (C) A professional athlete.
    (D) A retail sales clerk.

(handwritten: ①流行: shopping has gained popularity among the wealthy in many countries. ②普遍: the popularity of baseball ③聲望: The singer enjoyed great popularity during the 30s.)

GO ON TO THE NEXT PAGE.

51. (B) What are the speakers discussing?
   (A) A road-repair initiative.
   (B) A bicycle-sharing program.
   (C) A health and nutrition seminar.
   (D) A workplace safety event.

52. (D) What does the woman say is part of the service her company provides?
   (A) Product samples.
   (B) Event tickets.
   (C) Drug screening. 審查；篩選
   (D) Local advertising.

*initiate v. 創始；傳授；發起
into go
   n. 初學者；新進者
   adj. 創始的；初期的
initiation n. 創始；發起
initiative adj. 自發的；率先的
   n. 起步；開始；計畫
initiator n. 發起人；創始者

Questions 53 through 55 *refer to the following conversation.*

M : Hello, ma'am. Thanks for shopping at Good Choices Supermarket. Do you belong to our membership rewards program?

W : Yes, but I forgot to bring my card today.

M : Unfortunately, we can't use your phone number because our computer system isn't working. I'm afraid I can't give you a discount today.

W : No problem. I understand. Oh, and I grabbed this bottle of shampoo from the shelf but I just realized I don't need it now.

n. 所有物；財產；所有屬物；親戚

M : That's fine. I know where it belongs. Now will you be paying with cash or credit?

53. (D) What has the woman forgotten to bring? ㄅㄧㄥˊ béong 屬於
   (A) Some coupons.
   (B) Some shopping bags.
   (C) A receipt for an item.
   (D) A membership card.

①關係/所屬 What political party does he belong to
②主權：These books belong to me.
③社交地位：This is a place where he doesn't belong.

54. (A) What problem does the man mention? *discontinue ⎰stop ⎰suspend
   (A) A computer system is not working.   ⎱end   ⎱abandon
   (B) A loyalty program has been discontinued. finish terminate
   (C) A manager is not available.
   (D) A product is out of stock.

55. (D) What does the man imply when he says, "I know where it belongs"?
   (A) A supervisor is not available.
   (B) An item has been tagged with the wrong price. *tag
   (C) He can tell the woman where to find an item.   n.① 標
   (D) He will return an item to the correct location.   v.①加標
                                                      ②(IT)盯梢的人 ②附加；添加
Is the moral tagged to the story clear?
③(D)尾隨
The dog tagged along after me.

財產目錄報告
存貨清單報告

M : Thanks for agreeing to review the inventory report that I prepared, Ms. Campbell. Since it was my first time, I wanted to make sure that I did it correctly.

W : No problem, Dave. Overall, you did a great job. The only thing I ask is that you add serial 連續的 numbers and descriptions to the equipment list. We'd like to have every major office supply itemized. down | scribe fully   write (F)

M : Oh, right. I'll work on getting all those details this afternoon. Is there an example of a report that I can look at? It would be helpful to see how it was done in the past.

W : You should talk to Randy. He can give you a copy of last month's report.

56. (B) What is the main topic of the conversation? *supply under | fill v. 補充; 供給
   (A) A broken equipment. n. 庫存; 補給品; 軍需; 生活費
   (B) An inventory report.
   (C) An office floor plan. → supply teacher = substitute teacher
   (D) A project deadline. → a large supply of shoes

57. (B) What does the man request? → supply and demand 供需
   (A) A different office.
   (B) A sample document. *scribe n. 書記; 作家
   (C) Additional paperwork. scribble n. 潦草字體
   (D) Extra vacation time. v. 亂寫

58. (C) What does the woman suggest the man do? script n. 手跡; 正本
   (A) Revise a schedule. scrivener n. 代書人
   (B) E-mail a description.
   (C) Speak with a colleague.
   (D) Organize some files.

W : I'm glad both of you could make it, Tim and Derek. The board of directors approved our plan to purchase new security cameras. So someone from Cascade Industries is coming tomorrow to deliver and install them.

Man US : We've needed to upgrade the system for a while now. The river fell in a series of cascades down towards the lake.

W : I agree. So Tim, I'll need some of your maintenance department staff to help with the installation. 陡峭的/階梯狀的小瀑布

Man AUS : No problem. I'll send a couple of guys over to assist. Will three be enough?

GO ON TO THE NEXT PAGE

W : I think so, Tim. Thanks.

Man US : I hope there will be a training session for my security team to monitor the new camera system.

W : Yes, Derek, there will be training. Archer Industries suggested next Friday for the training. Is that OK for your team?

Man AUS : Sure. How about 9 o'clock?

W : I'll call the sales representative from Archer right away to see if that works for them.

59. (A) What is the woman announcing?
    (A) Some equipment will be installed.
    (B) A security inspection will take place soon.
    (C) A policy has been approved.
    (D) Some employees will be terminated.

60. (D) What is being arranged for next week?
    (A) A company outing.
    (B) A job fair.
    (C) A board meeting.
    (D) A training session.

61. (C) What does the woman say she will do?
    (A) Visit a client.
    (B) Review a proposal.
    (C) Confirm a time.
    (D) Test some equipment.

Questions 62 through 64 refer to the following conversation and floor plan.

M : Welcome to the Pasadena Museum of Art. Can I help you find something?

W : Hi, I'm trying to find the modern sculpture exhibit I saw announced on social media. Can you tell me how to get to it?

M : Sure. We are here at the information desk. That's the Photography Atrium directly in front of us. The restrooms are there to the right. Go straight between them and you'll come to the modern sculpture. It's a large well-lit space dedicated for special exhibits. That's where you want to go.

W : Thanks. Oh! And is my ticket good for special exhibits?

M : Yes. Everything is included with regular admission at our museum.

(handwritten notes in margin)
* terminate v. 終結；期滿 adj. 有限的
termination n. 結束；末端
terminative adj. 終結的 決定性的
terminology n. 術語 study
boundary / limit
dedicate / proclaim 奉獻
有效：The license is good for one year.

*經驗 →不可數
經歷 →可數

62. (B) Why does the woman talk to the man?
    (A) To sell some equipment.
    → I don't think she has the experience for the job.
    (B) To inquire about an exhibit.
    → She has a lot of unforgettable experiences living in Japan.
    (C) To purchase a ticket.
    (D) To sign up for a tour.

63. (C) Look at the graphic. Where does the man tell the woman to go?
    (A) Photography Atrium.
    ✕ I have many work experiences.
    (B) American Art.
    (代表換過很多工作)
    (C) Special Exhibitions.
    (D) Restrooms.
    ✕ I have no experience.
    ∨ I am not an expert in this area.
    ∨ I don't know much about that.

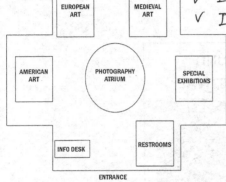

64. (B) What does the man say about the woman's ticket?
    (A) It can be purchased in advance.
    (B) It includes admission to special events.
    (C) It is issued only to museum members.
    (D) It is nonrefundable.

n. 保證人; 贊助人
sponsor v. 贊助; 主辦; 主持

Questions 65 through 67 refer to the following conversation and sign.

M : I think the bar is going to get a lot of good press by sponsoring the community art and music festival this weekend. It'll be a great way to get our name out there to potential new customers.
    PR 公關
W : It's certainly a good public relations move. Aren't you working in the beer garden the first day of the festival?
    因雨取消
M : Yeah. But if the event gets rained out and is held at a later date, I won't be able to work because I'll be out of town. The forecast is calling for thunderstorms this weekend, but I plan to be at the festival's opening day rain or shine. How about you?

GO ON TO THE NEXT PAGE

W : I'm scheduled to work the beer garden on Sunday, but I'll be there opening day helping a friend. She has a small jewelry shop and needs someone to handle the cash.

65. (D) Who are the speakers?
    (A) Community organizers.
    (B) Weather reporters.
    (C) Jewelry designers.
    (D) Bar employees.

66. (A) Look at the graphic. When will the man work at the festival?
    (A) On July 12.
    (B) On July 13.
    (C) On July 19.
    (D) On July 20.

SOUTHPORT COMMUNITY ARTS AND MUSIC FESTIVAL
JULY 12-14

Sponsored by Gilligan's Tavern
Rain date: July 19-21

Tavern
各棧；小酒館

67. (B) What does the woman say she will do?
    (A) Write an article.
    (B) Assist a friend.
    (C) Prepare some food.
    (D) Take some photographs.

Questions 68 through 70 *refer to the following conversation and product list.*

W : Hi, Joshua. It's Kendra Sheen. I'm calling about the tile options we discussed for my new bathroom.
    瓦

M : Hi, Kendra. Great to hear from you! Have you made a decision?

W : Well, I thought about going with the black mosaic, but then I took the samples into the
    馬養克
    bathroom as you suggested, and I changed my mind. I decided the color of the gray
    subway tile will make the room brighter.
    地鐵灰磚

M : Gray subway is a wise choice. It's cheaper than mosaic but just as durable, so it's good value, and with only one small window, the bathroom is already pretty dark.

W : Great minds think alike, Joshua! When could you give me a final estimate for installing the tile?

M : I'll have to crunch the numbers when I get back to the warehouse. Can I give you a call in an hour or so? 大約

68. (C) How did the woman reach her decision?
   (A) She did some Internet research.
   (B) She asked a friend for a recommendation.
   (C) She examined some samples.
   (D) She compared prices.

69. (C) Look at the graphic. Which product did the woman choose?
   (A) BM-0-99.
   (B) PM-0-98.
   (C) GS-3-52.
   (D) CB-1-83.

Tile Type	Product Code
Black mosaic	BM-0-99
Porcelain mosaic	PM-0-98
Gray subway	GS-3-52
Stone backsplash	CB-1-83

70. (B) Why does the man need to call back later?
   (A) He needs to check his work schedule.
   (B) He needs to calculate a price.
   (C) He is unsure about some inventory.
   (D) He is about to start a project.

GO ON TO THE NEXT PAGE

*stack v. 堆
n. 堆；堆疊
→ in a neat stack
→ stacks of money (D) 大量

PART 4

Questions 71 through 73 *refer to the following excerpt from a meeting.*

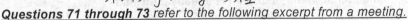

Thanks for the update, Rick. Now, before we close today's staff meeting, I have to announce an upcoming change at our facility. The building owners have complained about our habit of stacking empty pallets behind the dumpster on the loading dock. They believe it's a fire hazard and or could attract vandals. So from now on, all unused pallets must be stored inside the warehouse. Joe is building a rack in the shipping department which should be ready this afternoon, right, Joe?

*dump n. 垃圾場
v. 丟
dumb adj. 啞的
筆的

71. (D) Who are the listeners?
   (A) Guidance counselors.
   (B) Restaurant employees.
   (C) Bank tellers.
   (D) Factory workers.

n. 破壞他人/公共財產者
adj. 破壞文物的；野蠻的
jeopardy 風險；危險   peril
menace   威脅   → Icy roads are a peril to motorists.

72. (A) According to the speaker, what have the building owners complained about?
   (A) A safety hazard.
   (B) A broken gate.
   (C) Loud noise.
   (D) Discarded cigarette butts.

discard v. 拋棄；丟掉 n. 被拋棄的人/物

73. (D) What will happen this afternoon?
   (A) A new location will open.
   (B) A shipment will arrive.
   (C) Some training sessions will be held.
   (D) Some equipment will be installed.

Questions 74 through 76 *refer to the following broadcast.*

This is Rick Edwards with the WDGC-FM 100.3 health report. The Sharper Wellness Clinic announced today that they are conducting additional research on the effect of a sugar-restricted diet on motor skills in people 55 and over. Citing a need for more data on aging, they're inviting volunteers over 55 to participate in a three-month study. With me in the studio is Dr. Moira Clooney, director of the clinic. We'll be getting into the details of the study after this word from our sponsor, Jefferson Auto Repair.

conduct v. 領導；指揮；實施
引用
引~；鶴述
舉出

age bracket → 檔次
年齡層   類別   層級

motor skills 肌動技能 = 跳高、舉重
cognitive skills 認知技能 = 下棋；編寫計劃

60

74. (D) Who is Rick Edwards?
(A) A memory expert.
(B) An auto mechanic.
(C) A medical researcher.
(D) A radio show host.

75. (A) What are some listeners invited to do?
(A) Take part in a study.
(B) Test drive a new car.
(C) Apply for a job.
(D) Enter a competition.

76. (A) What will the speaker do after a break?
(A) Interview a guest.
(B) Make a special announcement.
(C) Play some music.
(D) Answer questions.

Questions 77 through 79 refer to the following advertisement.

When you buy a WaterKing, you're not just buying a dishwasher; you're joining the WaterKing family. And being part of our family includes the peace of mind that comes from knowing your WaterKing refrigerator will be serviced and maintained for the duration of its lifespan. WaterKing is unusual in the industry as the only refrigeration expert to offer a lifetime warranty on all its products. So come on, join the WaterKing family! Call us today to discuss your refrigeration needs. Mention this ad and receive a discount worth up to 20% off your next purchase.

77. (C) What is being advertised?
(A) A maintenance contract.
(B) A cutlery set.
(C) An electrical appliance.
(D) A mobile phone.

78. (A) According to the advertisement, what is special about WaterKing?
(A) It offers a lifetime guarantee.
(B) It ships internationally.
(C) It has won many awards.
(D) It has been in business for 50 years.

GO ON TO THE NEXT PAGE.

79. (A) What is offered for mentioning the ad?
    (A) A merchandise discount.
    (B) A complimentary service.
    (C) A product sample. *adj. 讚美的;恭維的*
    (D) A chance to win a prize. *免費的*

complement v. 補充;補足
n. 補語;補充物
compliment v. 稱讚;道賀
n. 恭維

Questions 80 through 82 *refer to the following announcement.*

藝術品
插圖

Good evening, ladies and gentlemen. I'm Sandra Liberman, events coordinator at Daisyfield Farms. Welcome to the Daisyfield Center Gallery. I'd like to thank you all for submitting artwork for our annual art exhibition. We're wrapping up the last minute preparations for the opening reception tomorrow evening. As you can see, the buffet tables are being set up as we speak. But we wanted to invite you here tonight to see your work before we open to the public. Additionally, each of you are entitled to 15 complimentary passes for tomorrow's reception. Don't forget to pick them up at the box office before you leave. If there are no questions, please enjoy the exhibit!

80. (B) Where does the speaker work?
    (A) At a radio station.
    (B) At Daisyfield Farms.
    (C) At a concert hall.
    (D) At a museum.

wrap up
① 包好;穿暖
② 掩藏: Why does he wrap up his meaning in such obscure language?
③ (Vi) 完成;結束: They wrapped up a couple of deals before lunch.

81. (B) What event are the listeners attending?
    (A) A farmer's market.
    (B) An art exhibition preview.
    (C) A dress rehearsal.
    (D) A company banquet.

④ (Vt) 總結;概括

exhibit
Vt / have
/ Ig'zIbIt /
exhibition
'eksə'bɪʃən

※ be entitled to 使有資格;給予權利
⇒ you are not entitled to sit here.

entitle v. 給權利;資格
⇒ The ticket entitles you to a free lunch.
⇒ He entitled the book "Harry". 命名

82. (B) What are listeners reminded to do?
    (A) Sign a waiver. *棄權聲明*
    (B) Pick up some tickets.
    (C) Respond to a survey.
    (D) Turn off their phones.

Questions 83 through 85 *refer to the following telephone message.*

Hi, my name is Ashley Walton and I'm calling about a camera I bought on your Web site yesterday——a Danton PK-900. My invoice number is 01127. So I've just received the

receipt n. 收據

camera and... Let me say first that I was delighted with the convenience of ordering from the site. The overnight delivery service was a bonus, too. However, as I unpacked the camera I noticed the instruction booklet is in Chinese! Anyway, I'm wondering if there's a link on your Web site to the English version of the instructions. If so, could someone send me the link? I would really appreciate it. My email address is included on the invoice. Again, that's number 01127. Thanks.

* parcel   carton 紙盒/箱
package   case 盒/箱
pack   packet 小包

83. (D) Where did the speaker purchase an item?
    (A) At a flea market.
    (B) At a department store.
    (C) From a co-worker.
    (D) On the Internet.

跳蚤
刺耳的話,責罵
it blame me
you come back
with a flea in your ear!

84. (A) What does the speaker imply when she says, "the instruction booklet is in Chinese!"?
    (A) She does not read or speak Chinese.
    (B) She did not know that the camera was made in China.
    (C) She ordered a different camera.
    (D) She would like to return the camera.

tempt = try
* tentative
                ㄝ ㄜ ㄧ
adj. 試驗的: a tentative plan
暫定的: a tentative proposal
猶豫不決的: a tentative smile/voice

85. (D) What does the speaker ask the listener to do?
    (A) Waive the shipping charges.
    (B) Ship a new camera.
    (C) Contact her by telephone.
    (D) Send her an e-mail.

= hesitant   = timid
= doubtful   = uncertain
= unsure   = undecided

Questions 86 through 88 refer to the following telephone message.

Hey Steve, it's Lorena. Did you get my email about tonight's award ceremony at the Lincoln Center? The event coordinator e-mailed me a seating chart, which I've forwarded to you. If you've had a chance to look at it, you'll see we're tentatively seated in the third row to the right of the stage. I know you wanted to be on the aisle in case we won an award. We have until noon to confirm or change our seating preference. Problem is, I'm on my way to the airport to pick up our associates from Dallas. So would you please contact the coordinator yourself? Her email address is included with the seating chart. Call me back if you have any questions. See you tonight.

aisle seat
window seat

* prefer v. 較喜歡; 提出   preferential
preferable adj. 較合意的; 較好的   adj. 優先的; 優惠的
preference n. 偏心; 選擇; 優先   → Nobody is given preferential treatment
                                  in this office.   特殊禮遇

GO ON TO THE NEXT PAGE

*orient n. 東方；亞洲 (Orient)；珍珠美

adj. 東方的；光彩奪目的（東西）

⇒ The rising sun is orient in the sky.

⇒ The orient sun is so radiant.

閃發光的；燦爛

86. (A) What is the speaker calling about?
adj. 劇場的；誇張的
    (A) An awards ceremony.
    (B) A theatrical performance. 舞台演出
    (C) A new employee orientation. 新訓
    (D) A retirement banquet.

He has a very theatrical style of speaking.

87. (A) Where is the woman now?
    (A) In transit.
    (B) At home.
    (C) In her office.
    (D) At the Lincoln Center.

dramatic adj. 戲劇性的

⇒ dramatic changes in the international situations.

⇒ There has been a dramatic improvement in her condition. 她的健康有了驚人的好轉。

88. (C) What does the woman ask the man to do?
    (A) Prepare an acceptance speech.
    (B) Find a parking space.
    (C) Contact an event organizer.
    (D) Set up some video equipment.

financial adj. 財務的；金融的

Questions 89 through 91 refer to the following telephone message.

Heather, it's Darren. I hope you didn't get the wrong impression during our discussion of your finances this afternoon. You've accomplished so much, and I'm honored to be your financial advisor. To think that you started with one café three years ago, and now you have half a dozen locations across the city. Few people could have pulled that off. 成功/完 So, listen. The shrinking profit margin 利潤率 shouldn't discourage you. In fact, I think you should go to the Small Business Conference in Reno next month. I saw that there are ①底線 some fantastic presentations scheduled on the topic of managing your bottom line. ②帳本底線 ③結果

89. (C) What is the speaker following up on?
    (A) A sales call.
    (B) A conference reservation.
    (C) A financial meeting.
    (D) A legal matter.

The plan was difficult and risky, but we pulled it off.

90. (D) Why does the speaker say, "Few people could have pulled that off"?
    (A) To avoid blame.
    (B) To correct an error.
    (C) To show disagreement.
    (D) To offer encouragement.

91. (D) What does the speaker suggest the listener do next month?
    (A) Close a location.
    (B) Hire additional staff.
    (C) Sign a contract.
    (D) Attend a conference.

Questions 92 through 94 refer to the following excerpt from a meeting.

Before we wrap things up, I have an announcement to make. The ability to deal effectively with our clients is the key to our success. And I know we can always improve our negotiation skills. So our firm will be offering a strategic sales seminar on September 1. If you're interested, please sign up immediately. Registration will close at the end of this week, so we can get a head count. The seminar will be led by Rupert Force, the author of Ruthless Negotiation. We request all seminar participants to have read the book prior to the event.

* strategy n. 戰略；策略
  strategic adj. 戰略的
  = planned
  = calculated
  = deliberate 經謹慎思考的
  = tactical 戰術上的

92. (B) What is the topic of the upcoming workshop?
    (A) How to advertise on social media.
    (B) How to negotiate effectively.
    (C) How to develop a telemarketing template. 樣板
    (D) How to recruit qualified employees.

93. (B) What does the speaker say about registration?
    (A) It includes a meal.
    (B) It will end soon.
    (C) It can be done online.
    (D) It is free of charge.

94. (D) What are seminar participants asked to do?
    (A) Generate a client list.
    (B) Copy some documents.
    (C) Join an online discussion.
    (D) Read a book.

GO ON TO THE NEXT PAGE

Let's leave the matter as it is for the time being.

Questions 95 through 97 *refer to the following excerpt from a meeting and budget report.*

目前
暫時

Due to the construction of our new community arts center, the city has cut our budget for the time being. And so it's up to us to find ways of cutting costs. It's been

= postpone = put off = defer = delay

suggested that we suspend one of our most popular classes, which also has the

under I hang

highest operating cost. We would get flooded with complaints if we canceled that class. So, another option is to host a fund-raising event here at our soon-to-be former location. Sort of a going-away party to help cover some of our operating expenses. I'm asking you guys to help me come up with some ideas to bring such an event to life. So, take some time to think it over and send me your ideas over the next few days.

使甦醒
使成真

95. (D) Look at the graphic. Which class does the speaker say is most popular?
(A) Chess.
(B) Yoga.
(C) Karate.
(D) Painting.

＊ flood n, ①洪水;水災
㊁ a flood of letters - 大批;大量
③漲潮;滿潮

Annual Budget Report v. ①淹沒 ㊁充滿 + sunshine
③湧進: Letters of complaint flooded in.

Class	Operating Cost
Chess	$600
Yoga	$1600
Karate	$2500
Painting	$3200

96. (D) What solution does the speaker propose?
(A) Recruiting more students.
(B) Reducing staff.
(C) Increasing material fees.
(D) Hosting a fund-raiser.

97. (D) What does the speaker ask the listeners to do?
(A) Take a survey.
(B) Make a donation.
(C) Register for a class.
(D) Submit some suggestions.

*dampen
v. 弄濕；使消沈 = to dampen sb's spirits 掃某人的興
enthusiasm 潑某人冷水

And now, WKLO-FM Radio Kansas City sports news. I know everybody is excited about the championship basketball game between our hometown heroes, the Flyers, and the

(上)

Cincinnati Rebels tonight at Wexler Sky Chips Arena. And I know the big snowstorm has dampened some of your spirits. Even the championship organizers are advising people to stay home tonight. It's dangerous out there. But don't worry about missing out. The game will be broadcast on our sister television station, WKLO Channel 2. Coverage starts at 7:00 p.m. However, if you are going to try and make it to the arena, I'm told snow removal is ongoing and all parking areas at the arena will be closed except the lot accessible from Ashland Avenue. Please plan accordingly and of course, go Flyers!

移動；撤退；滑落；(律)移交案件

98. (A) What is taking place tonight?
    (A) A championship game.
    (B) A rock concert.
    (C) A holiday celebration.
    (D) A theatrical performance.

99. (A) According to the speaker, why should listeners watch a game on television?
    (A) The weather has made travel unsafe.
    (B) Tickets have been sold out.
    (C) The event has been moved to a different location.
    (D) The game is played out of town.

100. (D) Look at the graphic. Which parking area will be open?
    (A) Main Parking Lot.
    (B) Parking Lot A.
    (C) Parking Lot B.
    (D) Parking Lot C.

* Is the chicken hot? 辣?
I love hot food. 辣食物
May I have a cup of hot water? 滾 ✗
                        warm   溫 ✓

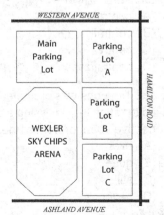

GO ON TO THE NEXT PAGE →

READING TEST

In the Reading test, you will read a variety of texts and answer several different types of reading comprehension questions. The entire Reading test will last 75 minutes. There are three parts, and directions are given for each part. You are encouraged to answer as many questions as possible within the time allowed.

You must mark your answers on the separate answer sheet. Do not write your answers in your test book.

PART 5

Directions: A word or phrase is missing in each of the sentences below. Four answer choices are given below each sentence. Select the best answer to complete the sentence. Then mark the letter (A), (B), (C), or (D) on your answer sheet.

①歡迎 ②贊同 ③樂於接受: I'd welcome a cold drink.

A 101. The board welcomed Mr. Tibbet's ------- regarding the parking situation at the processing plant in Folsom Ridge.
所有格+N
(A) suggestions n.
(B) suggest
(C) suggested
(D) suggests

A 102. Employees who fail to attend the safety training session on August 30 will be scheduled for an ------- date. adj.
(A) alternative adj.替換的=different n.選擇
(B) irreplaceable adj.不可替代的
(C) increased ⟷decreased
(D) unoccupied = vacant = empty

A 103. On January 10, Monolith Incorporated ------- shareholders of a proposed merger with the Termex Group.
(A) informed inform sb. of/about sth. 通知
(B) created to keep sb. informed of sth.
(C) announced+that~ 讓某人知道某事進度
(D) earned 宣布;聲稱

A 104. Johnson Airlines' first and most important mission is to ensure the ------- of all its passengers. +N.
(A) safety n.安全
(B) safe n.保險箱 adj. ①safe and sound 平安的
(C) safest ②as safe as houses
(D) safely ③a safe investment 穩妥的
④It's safe to say that~ 有把握的
⑤a safe driver 可靠的

14 → better safe than sorry
→ to be on the safe side
謹慎起見

A 105. The budget figures are reviewed monthly ------- Mr. Swift and the marketing director, Ms. Evans. 被者+人
(A) by prime adj.
(B) with ①首要的②最適合的③最好的
(C) to A prime site in the city centre.
(D) along prime quality 上乘品質

A 106. (DTV's prime-time fall schedule)------- reality shows, situation comedies, and competitive variety shows. S.⊕ v.
(A) includes ①競爭的②競爭性的③有競爭力
(B) include → by competitive examination 按考試成績分
(C) including
(D) inclusion → a competitive edge 有競爭優勢

C 107. Senator McGriff was a ------- figure in the effort to establish a state commission on tourism. stand 國家委員會
(A) centralize v.集中
(B) centrally adv.
(C) central adj.
(D) centralization n.集權化

D 108. Ms. Timmons was promoted to assistant editor after ------- missing a deadline in her five years of work at the magazine.
(A) even
(B) quite
(C) still
(D) never

This law is no longer effective. 生效的
② effective measures to reduce unemployment 有用的
③ an effective speech 精彩的 ④ to lose effective power 實際的

A 109. The Paris Rapid Transit Authority will
raise basic ----- on all bus and subway
lines effective July 1. *adj.*
(A) fares */ə'fektɪv/ /ɪ'fektɪv/ (上)*
(B) values *價值標準*
(C) outputs *產出;輸出;作品*
(D) assets : *she is an asset to the company.*
有價值的人
薩;優勢

D 110. Employees should report to their ----- *adj.+N*
supervisors at the beginning of each
work day to receive instructions. *報道*
(A) assigning
(B) assign *＊select*
(C) assigns *v. 挑*
(D) assigned *指派;分配* *adj 精選的,上流人士的*

A 111. Regular ads in select print publications
have ----- supported XYZ Inc.'s efforts *adv.*
to target the right consumers. *①.努力*
cess n. (A) successfully *①費勁: with/without effort*
cceed v. (B) succeeded *①成就: The book is her latest*
cessful adj (C) successful *effort.*
取就的 (D) succeed *④不遺餘力: to spare*
③最好評的;獲勝的 *no effort.*

B 112. Starting this Wednesday, Plectrum
Guitars ----- its store hours until 11:00 *校準*
P.M. daily.
(A) had extended
(B) will be extending *主動*
(C) will be extended *被動*
(D) was extending

A 113. The parking spaces ----- the front
entrance of headquarters are reserved
for senior management.
(A) near *①管理 ②經營 ③資方 ④管理人員*
(B) down
(C) between *⑤控制 + of stress*
(D) among *junior senior*
lower top +management
middle

B 114. Mr. Kalichnikoff suggested that he could
make ----- way from the office to the
new plant site without an escort.
植物 (A) him *①.*
工廠 (B) his *所有格 +N.* */ɛ'skɔrt/ n. 護送者*
(C) himself *反身代 N.* */ɪ'skɔrt/ v. 護衛;航*
移植物 (D) he *反身代 N.*

B 115. Since we have a few minutes to kill before
ending our session, Dr. Kevin Kelp will
speak ----- about his visit to Ethiopia.
(A) rarely *難得*
(B) briefly *短暫地; 簡潔地*
(C) recently
(D) slightly *輕微地*
＊incur v. 遭遇, 惹致
→ incur a debt 蒙受
陷於債務中

C 116. The company will ----- employees for
legitimate travel expenses incurred while
on official business. → *adj. 合法的; 合理的*
(A) reimburses *=legal =rightful*
(B) reimbursed *=lawful =allowed*
(C) reimburse *v. 償還;賠償*
(D) reimbursement *n.*
n. bag 自治區

D 117. Mr. Yarborough will be late for the
meeting this afternoon ----- his flight has
been delayed. *因為*
(A) why
(B) nor *conj. 也不*
(C) that
(D) as *介, conj. adv.*

B 118. Your new JP Four-In-One Printer will be
fully calibrated by a technician ----- *upon*
delivery and installation at your business.
(A) about *X*
(C) afterward *adv.*
(B) upon *介*
(D) next

B 119. Hartford Central Trust ----- a wide range
of services aimed at independent external
asset managers and their clients.
(A) buys *非銀行屬的財務管理人*
(B) offers
(C) gets
(D) comes

A 120. The shipbuilding firm of Melville & Noah
is seeking a summer apprentice with an *學徒*
strong drive ----- the craft.
(A) to learn → *a drive for/to V sth.*
(B) will learn → *to have a drive for perfection 追球*
(C) learning → *the drive to win 求勝的慾望* *＊義*
(D) learns

GO ON TO THE NEXT PAGE

D 121. Because graphic designers can ------- from collaboration, many firms find it helpful to implement an open office layout.

collaborate v. 合作

刊 n. 工具；器具；手段
v. 供給；實現

(A) help
(B) serve
(C) assist
(D) benefit

B 122. Due to a recent security breach of our network server, only authorized personnel have permission -------- the customer database.

n. 缺口
through /send

(A) accesses
(B) to access
(C) accessed
(D) accessing

n. 許可 permit n. 許可證
permit v. 許可
pretermit v. 忽略
pretermission n. 省略；忽略
置之不理

A 123. In ------- to your request, we have sent your Personal Identification Number (PIN) to the mail address listed on your account.

(A) response = reply = answer = acknowledgement
(B) responded
(C) respond = answer = reply to = acknowledge
(D) responsive adj. 熱情的，有反應的 + to a treatment

C 124. At Lexington Dietary Clinic, our focus is on giving ------- of our clients a personalized weight-loss management plan.

(A) whatever
(B) whose
(C) each
(D) every

盈虧帳目

D 125. This month's profit and loss statement will be delayed ------- the accounting department is still learning to use the new spreadsheet software.

(A) whether   宅腦程式
(B) so that   為的是；因此
(C) in case of   如果發生；假如碰上
(D) because

B 126. The supply of California avocados is expected to decline -------, so guacamole enthusiasts are encouraged to stock up now. → to be an enthusiast for sth.

(A) mainly   enthusiastic adj.
(B) soon
(C) eagerly   → to be enthusiastic about sth/
(D) ever   enthusiasm n. 熱情
              = eagerness = keenness

C 127. ------- after graduating from Ralston Institute of Technology, classmates Gary Winters and Michelle Kravitz confounded an Internet start-up company.

X (A) Despite 介 儘管
X (B) Provided that 倘若，以...為條件 +完句
(C) Shortly
(D) As soon as

B 128. At the end of the month, entrepreneur /ɑntrəprə'nɜ/ 企業家
Sophia Tang ------- her third and final lecture on digital marketing for mobile devices. 行動裝置

(A) to give
(B) will be giving
(C) giving
(D) may have gave → He is a man of great enterprise. 有進取

'enterprise n. 事業(有風) 企業；進取
精神

C 129. Employee morale at Starboard Global's Lexington office has ------- improved since Kyle Farmer took over as branch manager.   take over from sb. 接替某人
                                   as sth. 接任某職務
(A) notices
(B) noticing
(C) noticeably 明顯地
(D) notice   noticeable adj. It is noticeable that
              顯而易見的

A 130. Sparky's World of Toys and Games is looking for a part-time assistant manager to oversee the second ------- on weekends from 12:00 to 8:00 P.M.

(A) shift
(B) effect
(C) practice
(D) chance

Directions: Read the texts that follow. A word or phrase is missing in some of the sentences. Four answer choices are given below each of the sentences. Select the best answer to complete the text. Then mark the letter (A), (B), (C), or (D) on your answer sheet.

Questions 131-134 refer to the following instructions.

Backing Up Your Data

The IT Department recommends that you take the

precaution of ------- backing up your data and settings.
131.

------- manually copy your files to a network location or to
132.

removable media on a computer, click the Start button,

click Computer and then double-click the drive where the

files are located. -------. Copy the necessary folders -------
133. 134.

to a network location or to removable media.

有連貫, 枱理

131. (A) exactly
(B) regularly
(C) only
(D) softly

132. (A) To
(B) For
(C) On
(D) As

133. (A) Open the Users folder, and then open the user folder that contains the files that you want to back up
(B) Employees must log out of company computers at the end of the day
(C) You will receive an e-mail when software updates are available
(D) The (IT) Department is located on the basement of Building A *information technology*

134. (A) at the login page
(B) with the browser window 瀏覽器視窗
(C) on the mouse pad
(D) from the user folder

From:	ari_stiller@xcircuit.com
To:	ethan_hewett@crytpocon.org
Re:	Touching Base
Date:	October 13

Dear Ethan,

I was very pleased to meet you ------- the technology conference
135.
last month, and I'm sorry it took me so long to get back to you.

I enjoyed your presentation and I ------- your ideas intriguing. As
136.
I mentioned when we met, I would be interested in flying you

out to our headquarters in Phoenix to meet with our top-level

developers.

Of course, you are welcome to visit at your -------. Perhaps we
137.

can settle on a suitable date in April, if your schedule allows.

-------. Please let me know if we can talk by phone as soon as
138.

possible.

Sincerely,
Ari Stiller
President, X Circuit Media

(handwritten annotations:)

※ intrigue v. 引起注意
intriguing adj. 引起注意的/興趣的
an intriguing { smile / though / story

↑ pt
pt

convenience

find
keep + O + adj
leave { VPP (表O,被~) → He left his lunch unfinished.
V-ing (表O,發出動作) → Why did you leave the computer running all day?

---

135. (A) for
(B) among
(C) into
(D) at

(marked D)

136. (A) found
(B) will find
(C) is finding
(D) would have found

(marked A)

137. (A) significance n. 重要性
(B) convenience
(C) difficulty n. 困難 { financial / labor difficulties 財政困難 勞工紛紛
(D) account

(marked B)

I had difficulty in getting in

138. (A) I am enjoying the conference very much touch with him
(B) The launch is scheduled for early May
(C) It would be no problem to include the date
you requested
(D) Again, I apologize for taking so long to get
back to you

(marked D)

apologize to sb. for sth. ⇒ apologist n. 辯護者
off speak for sth. ⇒ apologue n. 教訓
v. 道歉 V-ing 寓言

Questions 139-142 refer to the following letter.

Timothy McNeil
1200 South Roosevelt Road
Omaha, NE 68786

Dear Mr. McNeil,

*lead to ① 通往某月的地
② 導致: What does this lead to?

The Festival of Lights Parade this Saturday night will lead to the closure
of Main and St. Joseph Streets to parking and through-traffic to make

way for the annual caravan of lighted floats. -------.   木筏: 花車
                 商隊, 車隊   139.   有ice cream 的飲料

Omaha Street and Mt. Rushmore Road will remain open ------- the parade.
                                                          140.

We apologize for the inconvenience. As the Festival of Lights Parade

becomes adv. -- popular, your cooperation is essential to its success. It
         141.

------- promote tourism, and thus, local businesses will benefit from the
142.
event.

For more information, please visit www.festivaloflights.com

Regards,
Owen Smalls
Organizer, Festival of Lights Omaha

---

139. (A) The deadline for registration is July 1 and
classes begin July 20
(B) After 5 p.m., no through traffic will be allowed
on Main and St. Joseph streets from East
Boulevard to Seventh Street
(C) This is to insure the safety of all volunteers and
marathon participants, as well as spectators
(D) We thank you for volunteering to assist with the
festival

140. (A) upon 介, 在以之上
(B) nevertheless adv. 仍然; 不過; 然而 Neverless, thank you for giving it.
(C) within 介, 在以範圍之内: They finished the house within an hour.
(D) throughout 介, 遍及; 貫穿

We can't act on your advice.

141. (A) increase
(B) increased
(C) increasing
(D) increasingly

142. (A) to help
(B) was helping
(C) will help
(D) had helped

GO ON TO THE NEXT PAGE

19

*ask 及物 ①.問→He asked him his name.
→He asked me where Tom was.

②請求;准許→He asked that they (should) be allowed
要求 to use a dictionary.

③素價→They asked 20 dollars for it.
→I come to ask you a favor.

Questions 143-146 refer to the following e-mail. *ask ①問候 +about
很物
③要求;請求 + for

From:	Rowan Brooks <rowan@brooksbeer.com>
To:	Anders Ahlgren <AA69@svenskmail.com>
Re:	Thank You
Date:	May 24

Dear Mr. Ahlgren,

Thank you for joining my Beer of the Month Club. I hope you
are enjoying this month's beer, Dreisel Harwin IPA. If so, I
would ask (up) you ------- a positive review on my Web site. 要是這樣的話
相反地 **143.** adj.作為號召的;作為特色的 等於
Conversely, if a featured beer does not meet your expectations,
-------, please let me know so I can improve my selection process.
144.
Any and all ------- is very important to the success of the Club.
145.

-------. Beer is something that I am passionate about, and
146.
running the club is just a hobby. I rely on members like you to
spread the word and to help me continually introduce new beers
to the world-wide community of beer lovers.

Sincerely,
Rowan Brooks
Brooks' Beer of the Month Club

口耳相傳
傳遞出去

D **143.** (A) will write
(B) writes
(C) to be written
(D) to write

A

D **144.** lack of +N 候款/價格 (A) for lack of a better term
(B) without a warning
(C) given the doubt
(D) by all means

adj.規定的 You have to finish the work
指定的 in a given time.

n.已知的事實 It is taken as a given.
介.如果有,假如 + that

145. (A) feedback
(B) evidence
(C) medium
(D) production

v.容納;接待 大量的訂單
D **146.** (A) Although I keep a wide variety of beers in
stock, I cannot accommodate bulk orders
(B) I apologize if there was a delay in shipping
your order
(C) My products are also distributed to many
national restaurant chains
(D) As stated on my Web site, I am not a
commercial retailer
商業的;商業廣告的;營利本位的

20

Directions: In this part you will read a selection of texts, such as magazine and newspaper articles, e-mails, and instant messages. Each text or set of texts is followed by several questions. Select the best answer for each question and mark the letter (A), (B), (C), or (D) on your answer sheet.

Questions 147-148 refer to the following Web page.

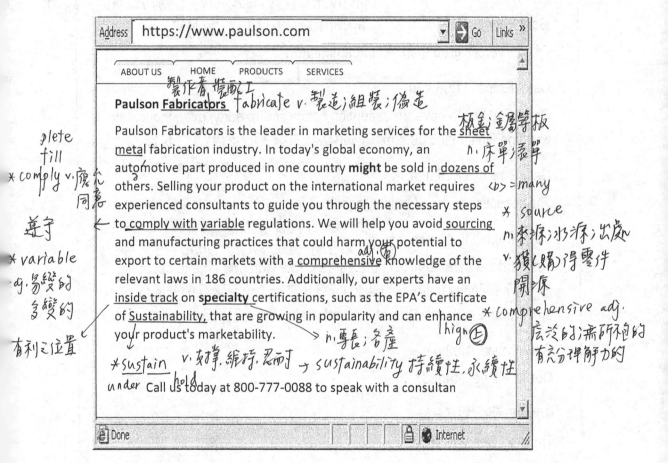

Address https://www.paulson.com

ABOUT US   HOME   PRODUCTS   SERVICES

Paulson Fabricators

Paulson Fabricators is the leader in marketing services for the sheet metal fabrication industry. In today's global economy, an automotive part produced in one country **might** be sold in dozens of others. Selling your product on the international market requires experienced consultants to guide you through the necessary steps to comply with variable regulations. We will help you avoid sourcing and manufacturing practices that could harm your potential to export to certain markets with a comprehensive knowledge of the relevant laws in 186 countries. Additionally, our experts have an inside track on **specialty** certifications, such as the EPA's Certificate of Sustainability, that are growing in popularity and can enhance your product's marketability.

Call us today at 800-777-0088 to speak with a consultan

Done   Internet

147. Who will the customers of Paulson Fabricators most likely be?
(A) Assembly line supervisors.
(B) Automobile dealers.
(C) Construction workers.
(D) Sheet metal fabricators.

148. What is NOT mentioned as a strength of Paulson Fabricators?
(A) Highly experienced employees.
(B) Knowledge of market trends.
(C) Expertise in advertising campaigns.
(D) Familiarity with legal matters.

GO ON TO THE NEXT PAGE

Carol Petrie 11:06 a.m.

Hi, Gary. I'm still at the bakery waiting for the cake to be boxed up for transport. The floor plan and instructions are on my desk. Can you start setting up the tables?

Gary Ponce 11:07 a.m.

Of course. I'll grab them and head out now.

Carol Petrie 11:08 a.m.

Great. I'd like to have the reception space set up early, even though the wedding isn't until 6:00 p.m.

Gary Ponce 11:09 a.m.

The reception is in the atrium, right?

Carol Petrie 11:11 a.m.

Yes, and the ceremony is in the garden. We won't be able to decorate for the ceremony until I get back, though. The flowers aren't due to arrive until 2:00 p.m. So just concentrate on the reception area.

Gary Ponce 1:02 p.m.

Got it. I'll get started.

Carol Petrie 1:07 P.M.

Thanks. See you soon.

149. At 1:02 P.M. what does Mr. Ponce most likely mean when he writes, "Got it."?
(A) He is positive that the information is on the desk.
(B) He is sure that Ms. Petrie chose the right tables.
(C) He is confirming the order for flowers.
(D) He understands Ms. Petrie's instructions.

150. Where is Mr. Ponce most likely going next?
(A) To an office supply room.
(B) To a flower shop.
(C) To an atrium.
(D) To a church.

The Campbell Conservation Federation 聯盟；聯邦政府（制度）

Seeks a full-time Field Assistant to aid our research

scientists with ongoing wildlife studies within the

Campbell Valley Nature Preserve. 保存；保護；維持

醃：preserve fish in salt

保護區

• Experience in wildlife data collection and in using
  advanced database software for record-keeping
  and generating reports is required.

• Candidates must also demonstrate familiarity with
  the common wildlife species in the valley region.

Certify a teacher 發證照   certify 證明,證實

• Applicants who are certified in wilderness first aid
  will be given special consideration.   荒野急救

• Minimum qualifications also include a bachelor's
  degree in natural resources, environmental
  studies, or related fields, plus 2 years of relevant
  work experience.

conduct v. 領導；指揮；傳導
conduct n. 行為

151. What is indicated about the Campbell Conservation Federation?
(A) It conducts research.
(B) It has advertised for a part-time position.
(C) It has relocated its headquarters to the valley. relocate 重新安置；搬
(D) It does not keep detailed records.

152. What is NOT a qualification for the position?
(A) Familiarity with computers.
(B) A knowledge of animals in the area.
(C) A college degree.
(D) Training in basic medical procedures.

* medical
adj. 醫學的；內科的
n. (口) 健檢
→ I have to have a medical before going abroad.

GO ON TO THE NEXT PAGE

n. 真空;吸塵器;空白;孤立的狀態.

Her son's death left a vacuum in her life.
Some people are living in a vacuum. 與世隔絕

V. 吸

```
DeWitt Supply Company
1040 3rd Ave South
Nashville, TN 37210
(800) 223-9980
```

```
Date: 06/05                              Time: 09:20
                        - SALE -
BSC2093    500 ct. 8"x6" Vacuum Bags                    $56.95
BSC4500    6" ARY Boning Knife                          $8.95
BSC4598    Bell Hog Scraper - Stainless Steel           $12.95
BSC8003    Rice Lake RS-130 Digital Price Computing Scale   $349.00
BSC9116    Custom Size Poly Board - 3/4" Thick          $25.00
Subtotal                                                $452.85
Tax (7.25%)                                             $32.83
Total                                                   $485.68
Paid by credit card          VISA xxxx-xxxx-xxxx-7734
A full refund is provided for all returns made within 30 days of
purchase with receipt.  Visit our customer service desk or speak to
our store manager for complete return policy.
*****************
Receive a 10% discount on a future purchase (of up to $100)
by sharing your opinion:
visit www.DeWittsupply.com/survey and use ID #BSC-KKD.
*****************
Thank you for shopping at DeWitt supply.
```

真空袋　考前臨時抱佛腳

剖刀;銼刀 → *He was boning up for an exam.*

a 抹�的種 cutting board 切菜板

C **153.** What type of equipment does DeWitt Supply Company sell?
(A) Electronics.
(B) Stationery. 文具
(C) Meat processing.
(D) Dry cleaning.

D **154.** According to the receipt, how can customers get a discount?
(A) By visiting the customer service desk.
(B) By making a purchase over $100.
(C) By speaking to the store manager.
(D) By answering an online survey.

*survey
①俯視
→ *You can survey the whole city from here.*

② 審視;檢視;測量;調查
→ *She surveyed herself in a mirror.*

Looking for a unique and memorable experience? Something delicious and different? Then a New York Culinary Adventure Co. (NYCAC) food tour is the perfect choice for your group or special occasion. Experience the best foods in the city with our expert tour guides!

Every Saturday and Sunday from May through September, guests will take a guided walking tour of restaurants in the downtown area. Every restaurant that we will visit is featured in the respected Nugent's Fine Dining Guide to the East Coast.

On the tour, guests will:

• Take a guided walking tour in Manhattan
• Sample delicious appetizers and tasting plates of signature dishes at five different restaurants, all within walking distance of each other
• Receive an NYCAC tote bag filled with restaurant coupons, recipe cards, and sweet treats from each restaurant on the tour

The cost is $195 for Saturday tours and $185 for Sunday tours. Tours run from 5:30 p.m. to 10:00 p.m. Each tour requires a minimum of ten guests. Guests should be prepared for up to two hours of moderately paced walking.

For more information about participating restaurants, or to book a tour, visit www.nycac.com.

155. What is being advertised?
(A) A recently published dining guide.
(B) A discount on a cooking class.
(C) A restaurant.
(D) A special tour.

156. What are participants expected to do?
(A) Arrive twenty minutes early.
(B) Give feedback about food.
(C) Order food in advance.
(D) Walk for an extended period of time.

157. What is indicated about the restaurants featured in NYCAC food tours?
(A) They take reservations online.
(B) They operate in several cities.
(C) They have been featured in a guide.
(D) They run daily events.

GO ON TO THE NEXT PAGE

Robertson & Baldwin Awards Dinner

The Robertson & Baldwin's awards dinner will take place as planned on Friday, December 3, commencing at 6:00 p.m. However, the event location has been changed due to water damage caused by the recent storm. It will no longer be held at Le Monde Monique, but at the Sanderling Ballroom in Hotel J on Chapel Hill Avenue.

Directions from R&B headquarters:

Head south on 12th Street, which turns into Axelrod Road. Make a right at Peach Street, continue on for six blocks and then turn left at Chapel Hill Avenue. Hotel J is immediately on your right. The Sanderling Ballroom is located on the main floor off the lobby.

Parking information:

Parking is available at Hotel J in a private area. The entrance to the area is to the right of the building. To avoid paying a fee, please bring your awards dinner invitation to show the parking attendant.

---

158. What has been changed about the event?
(A) The time.
(B) The place.
(C) The date.
(D) The price.

159. Where is Robertson & Baldwin's headquarters located?
(A) On 12th Street.
(B) On Axelrod Road.
(C) On Peach Street.
(D) On Chapel Hill Avenue.

160. What is indicated about parking at Hotel J?
(A) The parking area is under construction.
(B) Employees can be reimbursed for its expense.
(C) It is free for certain visitors.
(D) It will not accommodate all the event's guests.

26

② She spends time nursing her father / baby / flowers.
照顧 餵養 培育

Rex Donofrio
1725 S Walnut Street
Springfield, IL 62704
USA

✱premises n. 房宅;辦公;經營場所 (連金部地基建築)
→ keep off the premises 禁止入內

✱nursing n.看護;護理;養育
+ home 照料老人/病患の地方
+ mother 奶媽 ≠ baby sitter
nurse n. 護士;理;照料
v.① 懷有,抱有(想法)
He nursed the dream of becoming a great writer.

June 17

Dear Mr. Donofrio,

This letter is to confirm your registration for the 6th Annual World Nursing and Healthcare Conference in Heathrow, London, UK. —[1]—. We have charged the full $2,500 to your credit card, which will cover the welcome reception and all conference sessions and relevant materials. When you check in, you will also receive three vouchers valid for lunch at any cafeteria on the premises. —[2]—. Complimentary beverages will be supplied throughout the duration of the conference.

Please note that your access package does not include the awards banquet planned for Sunday night. However, you can still register and pay for the event during the conference itself. —[3]—.

Enclosed are a conference program and a map of Heathrow for your convenience. We encourage you to consult the program in advance in order to select the sessions you would like to attend. —[4]—.

Thank you, and we look forward to seeing you.

Sincerely,
Liam Stevens
Conference Registration Coordinator

法 效

$2,500
adj. 封閉的 / an enclosed space / garden 空間 圍子 真s.
·are enclosed 拿到前面 倒裝 → 強調

✱有紙本一起寄出
attach — 釘在一起
enclose — 一起寄出 = Enclosed herewith are details of~ = with this letter

161. Why was the letter sent?
(A) To correct a pricing error.
(B) To confirm a travel itinerary.
(C) To announce a professional gathering.
(D) To acknowledge a payment.

162. What is Mr. Donofrio advised to review ahead of time? *be advised to 被建議*
(A) A menu.
(B) A schedule.
(C) A city map.
(D) A scholarly paper.

163. In which of the positions marked [1], [2], [3] and [4] does the following sentence best belong? "Individual tickets will be available at the check-in desk for $50."
(A) [1].
(B) [2].
(C) [3].
(D) [4].

MINNEAPOLIS (April 10)— Morganstern, the country's leading manufacturer of locomotive engines announced this morning that CEO Carolyn Shapiris will step down from her position. In her sixteen years as CEO, Ms. Shapiris led the company through its transition from producing high-end aircraft motors to making the most popular locomotive engines in North America. —[1]—.

By shifting the privately held company's focus from aeronautics to ground logistics, Ms. Shapiris helped Morganstern become a major player in the large-scale locomotive industry. As a result of the company's success, SPG Domine Ltd. paid an undisclosed sum for controlling interest last December. —[2]—. Current Morganstern V.P. of sales Jermaine Gorman will be assuming the CEO position. —[3]—.

In addition to the change in CEO, Rajit Kumar is being moved from chief revenue officer to president, and Aldous Magnotti is being promoted to vice president of global manufacturing. The changes are due to take place sometime between the third and fourth quarters of this year.

After stepping down as CEO, Ms. Shapiris will lead a new corporate initiative with Morganstern's parent company. —[4]—. In the coming months, SPG Domine will disclose more information on its Web site as to exactly what her responsibilities will be.

164. What is the purpose of the article?
(A) To publicize job openings at a local company.
(B) To advertise new products being made by a company.
(C) To announce a change in a company's leadership.
(D) To report on a company's international expansion.

165. According to the article, what is Ms. Shapiris credited with doing?
(A) Increasing inventory.
(B) Lowering prices.
(C) Expanding the domestic market.
(D) Transitioning from one product to another.

166. What is indicated about Morganstern?
(A) Its sales revenue doubled.
(B) It opened a new training facility.
(C) Its employee recruitment process changed.
(D) It was acquired by another company.

167. In which of the positions marked [1], [2], [3] and [4] does the following sentence best belong?
"Details about the new position have yet to be released."
(A) [1].
(B) [2].
(C) [3].
(D) [4].

From:	James Booker <james@millenium.com>
To:	Olivia Wooden <olivia@millenium.com>
Re:	Property Updates
Date:	July 1

Hi Olivia,

Thank you for taking over from Cheryl for the next two weeks while she subbing for Jeff Kipps at our Peoria office. When Jeff suddenly fell ill, Cheryl was getting ready to market and advertise two homes in our region. She left me some information about the properties that I want to share with you.

The first is a five-bedroom, three-bath home located at 1228 Timber Creek Road in Decatur Heights. It comes furnished with modern appliances and furniture. Because it is so close to Lake Decatur and is surrounded by mountains, it has primarily been used as a vacation home.

The other property is 6915 South Clinton Street, here in Bloomington. It is a three-bedroom brick home with an attached two-car garage. It was renovated eight months ago and has new kitchen appliances but is otherwise unfurnished. It has a large, fenced-in backyard and a spacious wooden deck that is quite suitable for hosting parties.

Cheryl was in a rush to catch her flight to Peoria, and failed to mention the listing price of both properties. You'll need to contact her for that information, as well as any other details you might deem relevant. These and some other properties currently in our portfolio must be advertised early next week, both on our Web site and in the local paper.

James

GO ON TO THE NEXT PAGE.

168. Why was the e-mail sent?
  (A) To propose a new marketing campaign.
  (B) To give information about two properties.
  (C) To provide an update on contract negotiations.
  (D) To request that some information be sent to a client.

169. What is suggested about Cheryl?
  (A) She will be out of the Bloomington office for the rest of the year.
  (B) She is filling in a for a sick colleague.
  (C) She frequently goes to Peoria.
  (D) She owns two homes.

170. What is NOT mentioned about the property on South Clinton Street?
  (A) It has an enclosed yard.
  (B) It has a space for hosting social events.
  (C) It has been furnished with new (kitchen) appliances.
  (D) It has been on the market for eight months.

171. According to the e-mail, what is indicated about the Web site of Millennium Real Estate?
  (A) It will feature the properties Ms. Wooden must advertise. 查不到的；難達成的
  (B) It will briefly be inaccessible to the public the following week.
  (C) It features testimonials from the company's clients.
  (D) It lists properties not advertised in newspapers.

★testimonial n.證明書；獎狀
witness adj.證明的
感謝的
testimony n.證言；口供

Questions 172-175 refer to the following letter.

The manager was found to have appropriated store money. 挪用

appropriate adj. 適合的；適當的 to proper
v. 擅用；據為己有；撥款

City of El Paso
Department of Revenue
Commissioner Andrea Juarez
1 Commerce Plaza
El Paso, TX 79901

Dear Mr. Diaz,

prominent = noticeable = obvious = outstanding = conspicuous

⇒ The city will appropriate funds for the new project.
⇒ appropriation n. 擅用；撥款
⇒ appropriator n. 擅用者；佔用者

Congratulations! Your application for a building permit has been approved and enclosed with this letter. Please be reminded that the permit must be displayed in a prominent location where the work is taking place and be clearly visible to inspectors. Now that you have received your building permit, please visit our Web site (http://www.elpaso.gov/index) to complete and submit the appropriate tax electronically. Once approved (the process takes less than 10 minutes) you are authorized to collect taxes. Please be aware that if you do not file a business tax form within 15 days of receiving your permit, you will be ordered to pay a fine of $500 per day, and your license may be suspended for up to 10 business days, or until the tax form is filed.

forward
see 人 Inspect 檢查

Thank you for doing business in the city of El Paso. If you still need some help or have questions, feel free to give us a call at 915-234-1880.

Sincerely
Andrea Juarez
Commissioner of Revenue

impose v. 課稅，加負擔於 ~ on/upon
put
打擾：I don't want to impose on you by staying too long.
欺騙：She knows she was imposed on. 知道自己上當.

172. What information is announced in the letter?
(A) A license has been issued.
(B) A fine was imposed in error.
(C) An office has been moved.
(D) A new tax law has been passed.

173. What does Ms. Juarez ask Mr. Diaz to do?
(A) Pay a processing fee.
(B) Contact a local office.
(C) Approve a request.
(D) Submit a form.

174. The second paragraph, line 4, the word "authorized" is closest in meaning to?
(A) Undecided.
(B) Organized.
(C) Purchased.
(D) Empowered.

175. Which of the following is NOT mentioned in the letter?
(A) Instructions for displaying the license.
(B) Possible penalties for failure to submit a form.
(C) The type of business owned by Mr. Diaz.
(D) Ms. Juarez's official title.

GO ON TO THE NEXT PAGE

expo exposition ①,展覽會 ②說明: This is a clear exposition of the theory of evolution.
out put = explanation
expositor n. 解釋者, 註解者

Questions 176-180 refer to the following flyer and e-mail.

AIA USA's 21st annual Automotive Expo and Trade Fair, August 1-4

GM Renaissance Center, Detroit, Michigan

/rɛnə'zans /n. 文藝復興 /rɪ'nesns/ n. 新生; 復活

AIA USA (Automotive Industry Association USA) invites companies to support its trade fair. More exhibitors than ever before have attracted more visitors than ever before. Almost 40,000 attendees! The need for better, faster, more accurate component and full-vehicle test and validation technologies is clearly greater than ever.

val, vai = strong = worth

valid adj. 有效的 正確的

AIA USA is pleased to offer the following levels of corporate sponsorships with corresponding benefits.

'validate v., v. 確認

with back pledge 把V變成adj.

cry → crying   * correspond v. 符合; 相稱
forgive → forgiving   correspondent adj. 符合的; 一致的

validation n. 確認

For inquiries, contact Mr. Dale Whiteside, at 404-972-9333 ext. 8.

To register, email: sponsors@aia-usa.org

correspondence n. 一致

va|idity n. 效力, 正當性

Enterprise Patron - $1,750 per attendee

企業 支所

Representatives of your company will have the honor of attending the AIA USA Awards Gallery Opening Ceremony on August 1.

Merchant Patron $2,000 (LIMITED AVAILABILITY)

零售商 部

There will be up to 50 mobile-device charging stations posted throughout the event center, each sponsored by a Merchant Patron company.

可動裝置

Platinum Patron $3,500

白金

Your company's logo will be included on all fabric tote bags, to be distributed to every visitor.

織品; 布料

Executive Patron $5,000

經理/主管

Two executives of your company will attend the AIA USA Gala Banquet on the closing night of the expo, August 4.

32

From: sponsors@aia-usa.org
To: chase_k@daytrak.com
Date: July 15
Subject: Thank you

*process
| cede, ceed = go
n. 進行; 過程 v. 加工, 處理 (processed food 加工食品)
process v. 列隊前進

Dear Mr. Chase,

incorporated

Thank you for registering Daytrak Instruments Inc. as a sponsor of the Automotive Industry Association's 21st Expo and Trade Fair. Your sponsorship not only helps to make this year's event possible, but also to generate interest in your products.

Your patronage of $5,000 has been processed. Additionally, we are offering you sponsorship of our expo bags at no additional cost. This offer is a token of our appreciation for your long-standing support of AIA USA and its program. To finalize the promotional materials, please send us a digital file of your company's logo.

資助, 光顧

模記; 象徵

存在久的, 長年的

Dale Whiteside, AIA USA Program Coordinator

C 176. What is the purpose of the flyer?
(A) To report on the itinerary of a marketing campaign.
(B) To encourage industry executives to support a charity project.
(C) To promote the benefits of participating in an event.
(D) To present a breakdown of the cost of hosting an activity.

故障
損壞; 破裂

A 177. According to the flyer, when should a call be placed to AIA USA's office?
(A) When additional information is required.
(B) When a change in sponsorship level must be made.
(C) When a contribution cannot be processed.
(D) When a payment has not been received.

B 178. What will happen on August 4?
(A) A product will be launched.
(B) A formal dinner will be held.
(C) Sales figures from last year's expo will be released.
(D) Mobile-device charging stations will be installed.

B 179. What is true about AIA USA's event?
(A) It is partially funded by the electronics industry.
(B) It is held in Detroit.
(C) It is intended to promote enthusiasm for motor sports.
(D) It attracts more than 40,000 visitors annually.

B 180. What is not indicated about Daytrak Instruments Inc.?
(A) It has paid to attend a banquet.
(B) It will install wireless monitoring devices in the exhibition hall.
(C) It has sponsored AIA USA's trade fair on various occasions.
(D) Its logo will be displayed on souvenir bags.

GO ON TO THE NEXT PAGE

Questions 181-185 refer to the following notice and e-mail.

(handwritten: electronic adj. 電子的 / electronics n. 電子學; 電子器件)

To all supervisors and staff:

As you know, Lambert's is the most trusted name in electronics in the state of Tennessee. However, our financial prospects continue to decline and it's time to shake things up. We have been in business for over 10 years. Just five years ago our annual sales were $35 million from our 12 stores, with two stores taking in over $10 million each.

(handwritten: 重新整頓 / 做重大調整)
(handwritten: n. 前景; 希望; 潛在客戶 前 see)

We all know that competition from big discount stores has severely cut into our sales. Consumers browse our merchandise, but end up buying at the discount stores to save a few bucks. Even when we have major sales and match the discount retailers, people still buy from them. Last year's sales dropped to just $25 million dollars for our 8 remaining stores. If we can't reach sales of $30 million dollars before this year's end, we will be forced to close more locations.

(handwritten: merchant n. 商人 adj. 商人業的 / severe adj. 嚴酷的 + winter 嚴厲的)
(handwritten: n. 商品(集N.) / cut into sth 切入; 切入河道)
(handwritten: trade) reward)
(handwritten: 配合 使致)
(handwritten: 剩下的)
(handwritten: reach out to sth 伸援手; 求助 / for sth. 伸出手)

On the advice of my sister, an economist at Business Weekly, I am reaching out to all of you for feedback on how to increase sales and save our stores. Please e-mail me your ideas or call my secretary to arrange a meeting.

Thank you,

Stan Lambert
CEO
Lambert's Electronics

*(handwritten: * economy n. 經濟; 節約)*
(handwritten: The employees of the firm practised economy in doing everything)
(handwritten: ⇒ economic adj. 經濟的, 有利可圖的 + contraction 緊縮 + downturn 衰退)
(handwritten: ⇒ economical adj. ①節約的: an economical car)
(handwritten: ②簡潔的: to be economical with words)
*(handwritten: * practise v. 練習; 從事; 實施)*
(handwritten: to practise as a doctor/lawyer)
(handwritten: practice n. 實踐; 練習; 習慣)
(handwritten: the practice of doing sth.)
(handwritten: in practice 實際上)

From:	Jeff Robinson <j_rob@rockmail.com>
To:	Stan Lambert <ceo_stan@lamberts.com>
Re:	Feedback
Date:	November 1

Mr. Lambert,

I have been with the company since the very beginning, and as a salesperson in the stereo department, I too, have agonized over the drop in sales. I don't have a college degree, but I realize that if we can't compete with discount stores, we will have to consolidate our operations. However, I can point to two areas of focus where we fail as a retailer. First, the big discounters have "no questions asked" return policies – and we don't. Sometimes people buy something, get it home, and it isn't what they wanted. Even my family buys from the discount stores for that reason alone. Second, we discontinued our used equipment program, which killed two birds with one stone. First, it allowed people to trade in and upgrade to a more expensive item. Second, people could buy equipment knowing they could return it for any reason. Thus, they were far more likely to make the initial purchase. Anyway, these are only my suggestions.

Sincerely,
Jeff Robinson
Stereo Department, Tempe Store

GO ON TO THE NEXT PAGE.

181. Where would Stan Lambert's notice most likely be seen?
(A) In a music magazine.
(B) In a company annual report.
(C) In a local newspaper.
(D) In a company newsletter.

182. What was Lambert's Electronics revenue last year?
(A) $25 million.
(B) $30 million.
(C) $35 million.
(D) $50 million.

183. What is the purpose of Jeff's email?
(A) To recommend more advertising.
(B) To criticize past management decisions.
(C) To propose new methods of promotion.
(D) To recommend changes in store policies.

184. What does Jeff think the main problem is?
(A) Discount stores offer more products.
(B) There are too many salespeople.
(C) Most stores are located in bad neighborhoods.
(D) Customers want an option to return merchandise.

185. What do Stan and Jeff agree on?
(A) Stores must be closed if sales don't improve.
(B) They should eliminate part-time positions.
(C) Trade-ins lead to upgrades.
(D) New stores must be attractive to younger customers.

make amends for sth. 賠罪, 賠償: Tim made amends to Tom for rudeness.
amend v. 修正; 修改; 改善 → amendment 修正案

AMENDED PET OWNERSHIP POLICIES AND RESTRICTIONS

ex | fault
out

Attention all Sierra Vista Garden residents, especially pet owners! Due to
an overwhelming number of complaints, the housing board has approved
a new ordinance concerning pets effective July 1st.

order n.

慣例; 法令; 條例 ordinal adj. 順序的   adj. 重要的; 主要的; 基本的

As per the ordinance: ordinal number 序數   cardinal number 基數

- No exotic animals allowed. Existing registered pets will be allowed to
stay. adj. 異國情調的; 奇持的 + species 外來種

- Animals must be leashed at all times when outside their owners' apartment
unit. This includes all common areas, hallways, stairwells, sidewalks,
etc. leash   n. 韁繩; 皮條
v. 拴住; 約束; 控制: He leashed his anger and did not say a harsh

- Dog waste is not permitted anywhere e on Sierra Vista Garden property. word.
Do not allow your dog to relieve itself on our landscape. Take it
somewhere else.   lev=raise   relief
light v. 減輕; 使減少; 免除; 解救 n. 減輕
- Cats are not allowed anywhere on Sierra Vista Garden property, other 救助
than confined to the owner's unit. 安心

降3   它心限制在

confine n. 境界; 界限 v. 限制
end

(F) Violators will first be warned then fined. Continuous violators will be
considered in violation of association rule 34.d and will be compelled to
sell their unit.
compel   v. 強迫; 迫使
drive

---

violence n. 暴力
violate v. 違背; 反; 侵犯; 擾亂
violation n.
'violator
lel   ≠ violet : She's a shrinking violet.
I   害羞, 怕見場面的人

GO ON TO THE NEXT PAGE.

*dishearten
v. 激勵, 鼓舞 = encourage = inspire
↳ v. 使沮喪, 使灰心, 使氣餒 = discourage = depress

From:	max_leopold@textmail.com
To:	admin@svgproperties.com
Re:	Severe Pet Policy
Date:	June 21

To Whom It May Concern:

I was disheartened to read the new Pet Policy posted in the elevator.

下定義

- Would you please define "exotic animals"? Does that mean anything that's not a dog or cat? Are goldfish considered exotic?

- What about Ms. Jasper's parrot? You can't make her get rid of that bird. It's not fair.

adj. 不穩固, 不確定的　*鸚鵡或鳥, 模仿別人的人*

- The housing board is on shaky legal ground here. Housing boards cannot add or change certain rules, i.e. association rule 34.d, without first filing an amendment with city regulators.

協定, 職望　*that is 換言之*　→ *管理者, 監管機構*

- As everybody knows, the 'overwhelming number of complaints' were from one disgruntled resident with a grudge against his neighbor. Why do we all need to be inconvenienced by one person's blood feud?

n. 壓倒, 淹沒　*上*　*/fjud/ n. 世仇 堅持高標準*　*He enforced high standards.*

- How, exactly, are you going to enforce the dog waste policy? If my dog stops to take a pee at the fire hydrant, is someone going to jump out from behind a bush and write me a citation?

實行, 實施, 義行, 強追 =　*扭了 = 消防栓*　*拉了*　*/sɪ/ 引用, 列舉, 傳票(法)*

I think the housing board has lost sight of its primary purpose—to serve all residents, not just the selfish interests of one.

＊feud v. 結仇, 爭吵

Max Leopold
Unit 34 Bldg. C

The two families feuded with each other for generations. 世代為敵

38

186. What will happen to frequent violators of the ordinance?
- (A) They will have to turn their pet over to authorities.
- (B) They will have to face the housing board.
- (C) They will be required to pay a security deposit.
- (D) They will be forced to sell their unit.

187. Why was the ordinance added?
- (A) The property failed a safety inspection.
- (B) Too many people have large pets.
- (C) There are too many pets and not enough owners.
- (D) There were a high number of complaints.

188. What can be assumed about Max Leopold?
- (A) He owns a dog.
- (B) He is a member of the housing board.
- (C) He is responsible for many complaints.
- (D) He doesn't get along with his neighbor.

189. What is the purpose of Max Leopold's e-mail?
- (A) To settle a dispute between neighbors.
- (B) To discourage residents from having pets.
- (C) To applaud the housing board's decision.
- (D) To question a new ordinance.

190. What did Max Leopold not understand in the notice?
- (A) The exclusion of existing registered pets.
- (B) The fact that cats don't need to be leashed.
- (C) The location it was posted.
- (D) The date it becomes effective.

*exclude v.

＊exclude
①. 不包含，排除在外
The club excluded woman from membership.
②逐出；開除

GO ON TO THE NEXT PAGE.

Idaho Power Company One Idaho Way

Portland, ID 97223 Mr. Roseanne Tally 22 South Brighton Avenue

Portland, ID 97201 Account Number NT-789-E-09 April 9, 2014

Dear Mr. Tally,

Idaho Power is committed to environmentally sound business

practices. That's why we've introduced our paperless billing system.

Paperless statements are a great way to stay organized. Instead of

receiving a paper statement in the mail, we'll email you when your

statement is ready to be viewed on Idahopower.com. It's fast and

simple. When you go paperless, no one can access your account

information by intercepting your mail or going through your

recycling. Signing up for paperless statements is an easy way to

make sure you get one less piece of mail every month. Signing up is

a snap! Simply complete the enrollment form on our secure Web site

(https://www.idahopower.com/paperless), or call our customer

service line at 800-888-0012 for assistance. Once registered, you will

be able to pay and view your bill, start or cancel your service, and

schedule appointments. Best of all, it only involves a few clicks of a

mouse, and it may save a few trees.

We hope you will take advantage of this opportunity.

Sincerely,

Angelo Diaz

Customer Service Manager

Idaho Power Company

Monthly Statement

INVOICE # IDP-098234

DATE June 3, 2017

TO

Mr. Roger Tally,

22 South Brighton Avenue

Portland, ID 72399

Phone 530-987-3331 | r_tally@sockmail.com

Description	Amount
Last payment received on May 15	-95.00
Next meter reading – **June 23**	
Current Charges	
Total Amount Due on June 22	65.00
Total	**65.00**

Make all checks payable to **Idaho Power Company**

Payment is due within 30 days.

If you will not be home on the meter-reading date, call 530-444-3333 or

e-mail: meter_reading@idahopower.com to schedule a meter reading on a

different date so that we will not need to estimate your changes.

THANK YOU FOR YOUR BUSINESS!

GO ON TO THE NEXT PAGE

From:	r_tally@sockmail.com
To:	meter_reading@idahopower.com
Re:	Reschedule
Date:	June 9

Hi. This is Roger Tally at 22 South Brighton Avenue in Portland.
I will be out of town during my next scheduled meter reading.
Would it be possible to reschedule for June 30? Thank you in
advance.

* specify
see | make, do v. 指定; 詳細記載

Sincerely,
Roger Tally

specific adj. 特殊的; 特定的, 明確的; 具體的

P.S. I can be reached at 530-783-4449 during normal business
hours, or 530-987-3331 in the evenings and on weekends.

191. Why was the letter sent to Mr. Tally?
(A) To suggest that he sign up for a specific plan.
(B) To advertise a local charity function.
(C) To explain changes to his service.
(D) To notify him of his updated account number.

n. 功能; 職責; 集會

192. In the letter, what is indicated about Idaho Power Company?
(A) It is launching a groundbreaking advertising campaign.
(B) It has reorganized its marketing department.
(C) It offers customers an alternative way to receive statements.
(D) It has recently changed its meter reading policies.

破土
up
adj.
替代的
依選擇的

193. What should Mr. Tally do if he decides to accept Mr. Diaz's offer?
(A) Schedule an appointment.
(B) Pay a small service charge.
(C) Mall in a copy of his most recent bill.
(D) Complete a registration form on a Web site.

194. According to the monthly statement, when is Mr. Tally's next payment due?
(A) April 9.
(B) May 15.
(C) June 22.
(D) July 1.

195. What does Mr. Tally indicate in his e-mail?
(A) He did not sign up for paperless statements.
(B) He wants to reschedule a previous meter-reading date.
(C) He was charged an additional installation fee.
(D) He was not able to pay last month's balance.

*president n. 總統；會長；校長

presidential adj. 總統的；總裁的 表面的；統轄的

SWANN HOTELS
WWW.STAYWITHSWANN.COM

* punctual adj. 守時的；1.8細的

punctuality n. 準時，迅速

punctuation n. 標點

punctuate v. 下標點

July 2

Melvin Polasek, General Manger
Presidential Transport
100 W. Jayhawk Boulevard
Lawrence, KS 59777

*dispatch v. 派遣；發送；迅速處理 n. 急件，快電

→ He dispatched an experienced worker to repair the damage.

Dear Mr. Polasek,

All of us at Swann Hotels Lawrence appreciate the professional services provided by your drivers to our valued guests. Time and time again, guests respond <u>favorably</u> to the punctuality of your service, the cleanliness and comfort of the vehicles, and the <u>professionalism</u> of the drivers. Likewise, Swann staff consistently praise the <u>efficiency</u> and consideration of your dispatchers.

adv. 贊同地，善意地 有利地

efficiency n. 效率，效能

efficient adj. 效率高的 有能力的 功效

appreciation = thankfulness = gratefulness

As a gesture of our <u>gratitude</u>, we would like to offer a gift certificate good for dinner for two at any one of our three <u>on-site</u> dining facilities in Lawrence. Enclosed are 70 certificates to be distributed to your staff. A Presidential Transport identification card must accompany the gift certificate when the bill is presented. The offer is valid until December 31. Please note that reservations are not required, but they may be <u>advisable</u> during busy times.

明智的 adj. 可取的 適宜的

advise v. 勸告

Should you have any questions, please contact me at 208-222-9999 or email: g_decatur@swannhotels.com.

advice n. 忠告

act on one's advice 按某人的勸告行事

With warmest wishes,
Gwen Decatur
Regional Director, Swann Hotels South Carolina

HERE'S A GIFT
CERTIFICATE FOR YOU

兑换

Redeemable at:
Swann Bar and Grill, Mr. Niko's Kitchen, Top of the World at 34. Please present identification when redeeming the offer. Valid until December 31.

AWARD AMOUNT
Complementary dinner for two (includes all food, beverages, and taxes; tip not included)

Presented To	Issued By
Jeff Walker	**Swann Hotels**

GO ON TO THE NEXT PAGE

From:	m_polasek@presidentialtransport.com
To:	g_decatur@swannhotels.com
Re:	A Wonderful Experience
Date:	September 5

Dear Ms. Decatur,

I just wanted to drop you a note to let you know how thrilled I was when my boss, Mr. Polasek, presented me with a gift certificate for your restaurants at the Swann Hotel. My wife and I have wanted to dine at On Top of the World at 34 since we moved to Lawrence last year, and I must say, we were not disappointed. The food was excellent, the service was superb, and the ambience was delightful. We really enjoyed the evening!

華麗的　　氣圍(很好的)

一流的　　atmosphere 氣氛 (可好可壞)

Thank you again!

棒極的的

Regards,
Jeff Walker

196. Why did Ms. Decatur write to Mr. Polasek?
(A) To request a limousine for a hotel guest.
(B) To thank him for picking up a guest from the airport.
(C) To express gratitude for his company's performance.
(D) To inquire about transportation services in the future.

197. What is mentioned about Presidential Transport vehicles?
(A) They are well maintained.
(B) They have been recently purchased.
(C) They carry up to 16 passengers.
(D) They bear the logo of the company.

198. In the letter, the word 'valid' in paragraph 2, line 4, is closest in meaning to
(A) good.
(B) reasonable.
(C) just.
(D) convincing. 有說服力的、令人信服的

199. Who, most likely, is Jeff Walker?
(A) A professional chef.
(B) A parking attendant.
(C) A hotel receptionist.
(D) A transport dispatcher.

200. What is NOT covered by the gift certificate?
(A) Taxes.
(B) Drinks.
(C) Tip.
(D) Parking.

Stop! This is the end of the test. If you finish before time is called, you may go back to Parts 5, 6, and 7 and check your work.

New TOEIC Speaking Test

聽力 5-5

Question 1: Read a Text Aloud

聽力 5-6

((5)) **Question 1**

Directions: In this part of the test, you will read aloud the text on the screen. You will have 45 seconds to prepare. Then you will have 45 seconds to read the text aloud.

As great as the Internet is for social-networking, there's an underlying issue of privacy which could have a negative impact on your job search. The method of vetting candidates using search engines is now widely used by recruiters and is seen as a quick and easy way to find out more about the people wanting to work for their company.

PREPARATION TIME
00 : 00 : 45

RESPONSE TIME
00 : 00 : 45

GO ON TO THE NEXT PAGE.

Question 2: Read a Text Aloud

《5》 **Question 2**

Directions: In this part of the test, you will read aloud the text on the screen. You will have 45 seconds to prepare. Then you will have 45 seconds to read the text aloud.

Probiotic supplements may be a growing trend among health-conscious consumers, but the tiny bacteria that have been stuffed into capsules and stacked on pharmacy shelves coexisted with us before we were even aware of them. These live microorganisms are akin to the valuable microorganisms already residing in our bodies, a vast ecosystem of microbial species, including bacteria and yeast.

PREPARATION TIME

00 : 00 : 45

RESPONSE TIME

00 : 00 : 45

Question 3: Describe a Picture

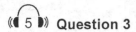 **Question 3**

Directions: In this part of the test, you will describe the picture on your screen
in as much detail as you can. You will have 30 seconds to prepare
your response. Then you will have 45 seconds to speak about the
picture.

PREPARATION TIME

00 : 00 : 30

RESPONSE TIME

00 : 00 : 45

GO ON TO THE NEXT PAGE

Question 3: Describe a Picture

答題範例

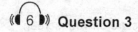 **Question 3**

Some men are on the side of a tall building.

They are supported by cables.

They appear to be washing windows.

They are wearing safety harnesses. 保險帶，顯

They are wearing safety helmets.

They are wearing tool belts.

The workers are at different heights.

The worker on the left is higher up than the other two.

All three workers are facing the building. rectangle 長方形 / right 角

The windows are made of mirrored glass. rectangular 長方形的

The windows are rectangular.

Some of the windows are larger than others. triangle n. 三角形 / triangular adj 三角形的

square n. 正方形(的) adj

One worker is reaching out to support himself.

This appears to be happening during daylight hours.

There are no reflections in the windows.

This is most likely an office building.

一致的，完全相同的

The workers are wearing identical shirts, which indicates they

work for the same company.

One of the windows appears to be slightly ajar. 半開著

72

Questions 4-6: Respond to Questions

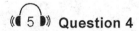 **Question 4**

Directions: In this part of the test, you will answer three questions. For each question, begin responding immediately after you hear a beep. No preparation time is provided. You will have 15 seconds to respond to Questions 4 and 5 and 30 seconds to respond to Question 6.

Imagine that you are participating in a consumer survey. You have agreed to answer some questions about your exercise habits.

Question 4
How much exercise do you get in an average week?

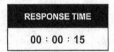

Question 5
What types of exercise do you most commonly engage in?

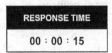

Question 6
Do you feel that you and your family get enough exercise? Please explain.

GO ON TO THE NEXT PAGE

Questions 4-6: Respond to Questions

答題範例

🎧 6 Question 4

How much exercise do you get in an average week?

Answer

> I go to the gym twice a week.
>
> I also ride my bicycle on a daily basis.
>
> I probably get about 10 hours of exercise per week.

🎧 6 Question 5

從事於，忙於

What types of exercise do you most commonly engage in?

Answer

> Riding my bicycle is the activity I do every day.
>
> I lift weights at the gym.
>
> I also occasionally go swimming.

ə e ə adv. 偶爾

occasion n ① 場合；時刻；重大盛典

起因 ② His departure was the occasion of much sadness.

理由 ③ You have no occasion to buy another car.

74

Questions 4-6: Respond to Questions

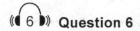

Do you feel that you and your family get enough exercise? Please explain.

Answer

as far as sb. be concerned
就此事與某人的關係而言

<u>As far as</u> my family is concerned, probably not.

Some of us are too busy to exercise.

I get the most exercise of anybody in my family.

頗為;相當地
My brother is fairly <u>active</u>.
adj. 活躍;活潑的

He plays basketball with his friends.

Sometimes he'll join me for a bike ride.

My parents don't get a lot of exercise.

My dad works two jobs, so he's always tired.

My mom has her hands full taking care of us, so she

  doesn't get much exercise, either.

GO ON TO THE NEXT PAGE.

Questions 7-9: Respond to Questions Using Information Provided

Directions: In this part of the test, you will answer three questions based on the information provided. You will have 30 seconds to read the information before the questions begin. For each question, begin responding immediately after you hear a beep. No additional preparation time is provided. You will have 15 seconds to respond to Questions 7 and 8 and 30 seconds to respond to Question 9.

deductible adj. 可減免的 可扣除的

deduct v. 扣除

(b)小孩

致富,豐富

Care and Share Foundation

Our members have been supporting our local food banks, homeless shelters, afterschool enrichment programs, Toys for Tots program and many other worthy community-based charities since 1978. Make Your Tax-Deductible Donation Today!

Pledge a donation at any of the following membership levels, and receive a thank you gift:

____ $20 Care and Share Membership (you will receive a subscription to our monthly newsletter)

____ $50 Care and Share Great Neighbor (you will receive a subscription to our monthly newsletter and a "Great Neighbor" T-shirt)

____ $100 Care and Share Community Leader (you will receive a subscription to our monthly newsletter and an "I Take Care of my Community" coffee mug)

____ $500 Care and Share Local Hero (you will receive a subscription to our monthly newsletter, a "Great Neighbor" T-shirt, and an "I Take Care of my Community" coffee mug)

We also accept donations of any other amount!

Yes, I want to support my local food banks, homeless shelters, afterschool enrichment programs, Toys for Tots program and many other worthy community-based charities by becoming a member of the Care and Share foundation at the $_____ level.

I want to make my payment using:

____ Personal Check (check # _____).

____ Major Credit Card (Type of Card: _____); Card # _____).

____ Please bill me later.

New Member Information:

Name _____ Phone # _____

Address _____

Grant Booker is interested in a supporting membership with the Care and Share Foundation.

PREPARATION TIME
00 : 00 : 30

Question 7	Question 8	Question 9
RESPONSE TIME	RESPONSE TIME	RESPONSE TIME
00 : 00 : 15	00 : 00 : 15	00 : 00 : 30

Questions 7-9: Respond to Questions Using Information Provided

答題範例

 Question 7

Hello, my name is Grant Booker. What is the minimum pledge to become a supporting member of your foundation?

Answer

> Hi, Mr. Booker.
>
> Thanks for calling the Care and Share Foundation.
>
> The minimum amount for a supporting member is $20.

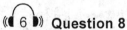 **Question 8**

What are my payment options for a supporting membership?

Answer

> We have three payment options.
>
> You can pay by personal check or credit card.
>
> We also have a "Bill Me Later" option.

GO ON TO THE NEXT PAGE.

Questions 7-9: Respond to Questions Using Information Provided

((● 6 ●)) **Question 9**

Can you tell me a little about the types of programs that your organization supports?

Answer

It would be my pleasure.

Care and Share supports a wide variety of programs.

Here are just a few.

We support local food banks and homeless shelters.

We fund afterschool enrichment programs.

We sponsor a Toys for Tots program and many other

worthy community-based charities.

*worthy adj. 相稱的；有價值的

Also, your donation is tax-deductible.

Any sort of help would go toward worthy causes.

目標；理想；事業；原因

Would you like to become a supporting member of our

foundation today?

World peace is a cause
we should all work for.

Question 10: Propose a Solution

((◀ 5 ▶)) **Question 10**

Directions: In this part of the test, you will be presented with a problem and
asked to propose a solution. You will have 30 seconds to
prepare. Then you will have 60 seconds to speak. In your
response, be sure to show that you recognize the problem, and
propose a way of dealing with the problem.

In your response, be sure to
- show that you recognize the caller's problem, and
- propose a way of dealing with the problem.

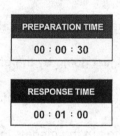

PREPARATION TIME
00 : 00 : 30

RESPONSE TIME
00 : 01 : 00

GO ON TO THE NEXT PAGE.

Question 10: Propose a Solution

答題範例

Question 10

Voice Message

Hello, this is Robert Potter. I recently purchased one of your Aerostar kits for my son, the supersonic jet model. Unfortunately, the kit didn't come with an instruction manual for putting the plane together. Now, I've bought a few Aerostar kits for him before and they've always had a full-color instruction manual inside. I've already tried to put the kit together myself just going by the photographs on the kit box. But it's almost impossible to get it fully right. Anyway, my son likes to put the models together himself by following the step-by-step guide in the manual. This was his main birthday present this year, so he's pretty upset about not being able to put his supersonic jet model together——sort of ruined the surprise for him, really. I hope you'll be able to do something about this as quickly as possible. Please call me back. This is Robert Potter at 955-7745.

Question 10: Propose a Solution

答題範例

Hello, Mr. Potter.

My name is Jenny Buechler.

I'm calling from Aerostar Model and Toy Company.

I'm sorry to hear about your recent experience.

I'm sure you must be disappointed.

I feel terrible for your son.

I'm going to do everything I can to fix the situation.

I've sent you the missing instruction manual.

The package was shipped overnight.

You should receive the manual tomorrow.

I understand how important it is.

I can only hope your son will enjoy his birthday.

In the meantime, I want to offer something as a token of our gratitude.

We value our long-term customers.

標記；表徵

We don't want to lose you.

Along with the manual I've sent a gift certificate.

It's good for one free Aerostar kit of your choice.

I hope you will enjoy it and continue to enjoy our products.

GO ON TO THE NEXT PAGE

Question 11: Express an Opinion

Directions: In this part of the test, you will give your opinion about a specific topic. Be sure to say as much as you can in the time allowed. You will have 15 seconds to prepare. Then you will have 60 seconds to speak.

It is often said that governments spend too much money on projects to protect the environment, while there are other problems that are more important. Do you agree or disagree? State your opinion and provide reasons for your view.

PREPARATION TIME
00 : 00 : 15

RESPONSE TIME
00 : 01 : 00

Question 11: Express an Opinion

答題範例

In today's turbulent economic environment, it is difficult for governments to decide which areas they should spend money on.

Some people believe that it is important to fund commercial development.

Others feel that it is preferable to prioritize environmental issues.

In my opinion, protecting the environment is more important than funding commerce.

For starters, environmental problems are a more urgent concern than issues surrounding the economy.

While we are certainly living in a society where the economy is important, the environment is a matter of life and death for many people.

The consequences of environmental degradation not only hit close to home, but also affect human beings all over the world.

① For example, within three decades certain countries in South Asia will suffer from catastrophic flooding as a result of global warming.

This means that nations in the developed world need to fund programs that will help them deal with the looming crisis.

② Moreover, while business development is necessary, it is entirely possible for economic programs to be privately funded.

Many businesses and individuals are willing to help entrepreneurs and new business owners.

③ Not only that, but the Internet has made it possible for small business owners to fund their projects through online "crowdfunding" promoted through social networking sites.

For instance, there is a community theater group in my hometown which recently lost a significant portion of its public funding following recent budget cuts by the municipal government. While the situation looked dire at first, the group was able to attract financial support from companies who wished to advertise on their programs.

In conclusion, I feel that if the government is forced to make a choice, it should choose to fund environmental programs rather than prop up the economy.

I feel this way because environmental problems are a more pressing concern, and because businesses can often be privately funded.

The environment does not have the same luxury.

GO ON TO THE NEXT PAGE

New TOEIC Writing Test

Questions 1-5: Write a Sentence Based on a Picture

Question 1

Directions: Write ONE sentence based on the picture using the TWO words or phrases under it. You may change the forms of the words and you may use them in any order.

bridge / collapse

bridge n. 橋　　　　　　　　　*The collapsed bridge is being fixed.*

v. 架橋於，縮短距離，便渡過
把…連結.(彌合)起來
Politeness will bridge a lot of difficulties.
禮貌會幫你渡過不少難關

collapse v. 倒塌,崩潰,瓦解.失敗,消沈,累倒
→ *The project collapsed for lack of money.*
→ *His health collapsed because of overwork.*
n. 挫折,突然失敗.暴跌

GO ON TO THE NEXT PAGE

Questions 1-5: Write a Sentence Based on a Picture

Question 2

Directions: Write ONE sentence based on the picture using the TWO words or phrases under it. You may change the forms of the words and you may use them in any order.

man / glasses

※ glasses
→ look at sth. through rose-tinted / colored glasses/spectacles.

過於樂觀的看問題。(太樂主法)

The mas who sits in the middle wears glasses.

Questions 1-5: Write a Sentence Based on a Picture

Question 3

Directions: Write ONE sentence based on the picture using the TWO words or phrases under it. You may change the forms of the words and you may use them in any order.

family / television

The family is watching television.

GO ON TO THE NEXT PAGE

Questions 1-5: Write a Sentence Based on a Picture

Question 4

Directions: Write ONE sentence based on the picture using the TWO words
or phrases under it. You may change the forms of the words and
you may use them in any order.

woman / transaction

*transaction 交易;業務;賣買
A→B | 另B

transform v.改變;改造

transport v.運輸,集送

The cashier completed the woman's
transaction in a matter of minutes.

Questions 1-5: Write a Sentence Based on a Picture

Question 5

Directions: Write ONE sentence based on the picture using the TWO words or phrases under it. You may change the forms of the words and you may use them in any order.

rocket / platform

There is a rocket launch platform.

* rocket launch 火箭發射

give sb. a rocket (口) 嚴厲斥責某人

* launch v. 及物: *The ship was launched today.*

船下水, 飛彈發射; 開始(戰事); 發出(命令)

開始: *We launched a new project.*

GO ON TO THE NEXT PAGE

Questions 6-7: Respond to a written request

Question 6

Directions: Read the e-mail below.

From:	Darla McIntyre (darla8923@gmail.com)
Sent:	Tuesday, July 24 12:32:16 PM
To:	Elaine Wang (elaine2389@yahoo.com)

Hi Elaine. I was wondering if you might be interested in a pair of tickets to see the ballet this Sunday. It's a performance of Swan Lake by the Geoffrey Ballet Company at the Royal Theater. The seats are on the main floor and the performance has received great reviews. Unfortunately, Don and I can't make it this weekend and I thought of you, especially since you're such a fan of ballet. The tickets are free, and think of it as returning the favor for getting us into the movie premiere last month.

Let me know ASAP if you're interested.

Best,

Darla

Directions: You would like to go to the performance, but cannot. Explain why.

Questions 6-7: Respond to a written request

答題範例

Question 6

Hi Darla,

Thanks for the offer. I'd love to see that performance——Swan Lake is my favorite! Unfortunately, I can't make it this weekend. Jack and I are driving the kids to summer camp, and we've rented a lake house up north. We won't be back until Monday. I'm going to regret it, but I must turn down your generous offer. However, I know Linda is very fond of ballet as well. Perhaps she is free this weekend. Thanks again, and let's get together sometime next week.

Cheers,

Elaine

be fond of 喜歡, 愛好
adj. 喜歡的; 溺愛的; 溫柔的
The fond father smiled
with pleasure.

turn down
①. 拒絕
②. 下降: The economy was
turning down at that time.

Questions 6-7: Respond to a written request

Question 7

Directions: Read the e-mail below.

From:	Julie Banks, Personnel Department
Sent:	Monday, April 5 4:41 PM
To:	Calvin Stelle
Cc:	Ron Kittle, Maggie White, main office
Subject:	Insurance claim #893

Dear Calvin,

I received most of the documents pertaining to your travel

expense reimbursement claim, but one crucial document is

missing: the flight itinerary from your trip to St. Louis. It's

listed on the report, but I don't have a hard copy. As you well

know, I cannot submit the claim to accounting without hard

copies of all receipts. Please submit a copy to my office at

your earliest convenience. If you have any questions or need

assistance, do not hesitate to contact me at ext. 9023.

Thanks,

Julie

[Handwritten annotations: pertain v. 附屬;有關 → We own the house and the land pertaining to it. 有關]

[Handwritten annotation: 賠償;補償]

Directions: Explain why you haven't submitted the required document.

答題範例

Question 7

Julie,

旅遊行程表

I didn't include a copy of the flight <u>itinerary</u> because I was never given a copy

following the trip. Maggie White booked the trip for me. I have requested a

copy from the head office at least twice. Ron Kittle told me that they would

forward a copy to you. Therefore, it's up to the head office to rectify this

situation.

矯正；改正

Sincerely,

Calvin Stelle

＊e-mail 補充

早期：As per our previous conversation

現在：As we discussed / As discussed

早期：Attached please find

Enclosed

太正式，很像律師信

現在：I'm attaching / Attached is ~

I've attached

GO ON TO THE NEXT PAGE.

Questions 8: Write an opinion essay

Question 8

Directions: Read the question below. You have 30 minutes to plan, write, and revise your essay. Typically, an effective response will contain a minimum of 300 words.

It has been said, "Not all learning takes place in the classroom." Compare and contrast knowledge gained from personal experience with knowledge gained from classroom <u>instruction</u>. In your opinion, which source is more important? Why? ㄣ、教學：命令；操作指南

→ She gives instruction in English.

→ Pleas read the instructions before drinking.

第一段：立場

第二、三段：原因

第四段：結論〈不要提出新論點〉

Questions 8: Write an opinion essay

答題範例

Question 8

The main difference between classroom learning and hands-on experience is fairly clear. The former teaches you to "think" while the latter teaches you to "do." Both are valuable in their own ways. For example, let's say someone is studying to become a teacher. Their coursework will teach them about teaching techniques and methods, but they won't really understand what it means to teach until they are given practical experience in front of actual students. In this way, it's very much like riding a bike. You could read a book about it, watch a video, learn every single mechanical part of the bicycle, but you can't ride until you actually get on the bike. I believe the same holds true for teaching.

Likewise, in many walks of life, you prepare yourself to engage in an activity by reading in advance. That way, when you're faced with the reality of the experience, you're better suited to accomplish your goals. At the same time, you will make mistakes and learn from them. Therefore, I believe both classroom learning and experience are essential parts of acquired knowledge. There are some cases where one is possible without the other, but for the most part, life is a combination of the two.